Please return/renew this item by the
last date shown to avoid a charge.
Books may also be renewed by phone
and Internet. May not be renewed if
required by another reader.

www.libraries.barnet.gov.uk

BARNET
LONDON BOROUGH

ADRIAN EDMONDSON

is an English comedian, actor and writer. He has three
daughters with his wife, Jennifer Saunders, and lives in London.
Tilly and the Time Machine was his first novel for children.

DANNY NOBLE

is a comic-making, storytelling, ink-based illustrator who
regularly falls off stages with her band The Meow Meows.
By day she wrangles five-year-olds and sharpens pencils.

She grew up by the sea with the most obscenely patient
and wonderful family and now she lives in the city
and swims with ducks.

Junkyard Jack

and the Horse That Talked

Adrian Edmondson

illustrated by Danny Noble

PUFFIN

PUFFIN BOOKS

UK | USA | Canada | Ireland | Australia
India | New Zealand | South Africa

Puffin Books is part of the Penguin Random House group of companies
whose addresses can be found at global.penguinrandomhouse.com.

www.penguin.co.uk
www.puffin.co.uk
www.ladybird.co.uk

Penguin
Random House
UK

First published 2018

001

Text copyright © Adrian Edmondson, 2018
Illustrations copyright © Danny Noble, 2018
Cover lettering based on a design by Lisa Horton

The moral right of the author and illustrator has been asserted

Text design by Mandy Norman
Printed in Great Britain by Clays Ltd, St Ives plc

A CIP catalogue record for this book is available from the British Library

ISBN: 978-0-141-37249-5

All correspondence to:
Puffin Books
Penguin Random House Children's
80 Strand, London WC2R ORL

For Fred, Bert and Ivy

CHAPTER

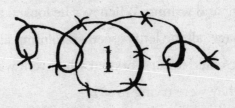

1

Jack was hiding inside his own school bag, which was hanging on one of the pegs at the back of the classroom. He'd climbed in during the lunch break and no one knew he was there.

You might wonder how someone could hide inside a school bag, but not only was Jack very small, he was also very bendy. In fact, he was double-jointed. This meant he could do all sorts of funny things, like bend his thumb back until it touched his arm, and lick his own elbows, and tie his legs in a knot behind his head.

Jack liked being inside the bag because it meant he didn't have to do any schoolwork. He didn't like reading and writing. Whenever he looked at words on a page, all the letters seemed to jump about, and he could never work out what went where, or what they were trying to say.

Jack could see through a little gap where the zip of his school bag was broken. All the other children in his class were sitting at their tables, writing about '*What I Can See from my Bedroom Window*'.

This was another reason why Jack had got into his bag: he didn't have a bedroom window. He lived in a cupboard. So the only thing he could possibly have written was *nothing*.

To be honest he was a little bit bored in his bag, but he still thought it was better than doing reading and writing.

The only interesting thing he had to play with was a small locket, which contained a photo of his mum. Looking at the picture made him happy and sad at the same time. He was really happy

whenever he saw her face, but also really
sad because he didn't get to see her
very often. This was because she was
in prison. She'd been sent there for
something she swore she hadn't done,
and Jack wished he could help her, but he
was only a boy, and he couldn't think what to do.

'Where's Jack?' came a voice from the front of
the classroom. It was Miss Tuppence, the teacher.
'Oh no, he hasn't gone missing *again*!'

Jack was always disappearing. During the
previous month Miss Tuppence had found him
hidden in the narrow gap between the whiteboard
and the wall; behind the bucket in the cupboard
under the sink; and in the drawer where she kept
the large sheets of paper for artwork.

'Come on, everybody – help me find him!' she
said, and the whole class scraped back their chairs
and started looking for Jack.

You might imagine that a game of hide-and-
seek in a single room with twenty-nine people

looking and only one person hiding wouldn't take very long, but it did. It went on for ages. And, as with any game of hide-and-seek when the hider is too good at hiding, most of the children got bored quite quickly and started chatting, and not looking at all.

Eventually someone knocked into Jack's bag. Jack froze. He looked out carefully through the gap between the zips. A boy called Archie had just banged into his bag by accident. But Jack knew they would find him sooner or later. It seemed a shame for them to discover his hiding place, because it was such a good one, so he decided to get out before they found him. Then he might be able to use it again another day.

As soon as there were enough children milling about near the pegs, he carefully

unzipped the flap, slipped out of his bag and slid down the wall behind all the coats. He was so silent and agile, and small and bendy, that no one saw him. Like a nimble ghost, he spirited his way past empty chairs and under tables, and swiftly scurried along to his own chair, climbed on to it and picked up his pencil.

'Where can he possibly be?' wailed Miss Tuppence, beginning to sound slightly tearful.

'Who is it we're looking for again?' asked a girl called Jade.

'Well, Jack, of course!' said Miss Tuppence, looking behind the whiteboard for the fifth time.

'But he's sitting right here, Miss,' said Jade, pointing at Jack.

Miss Tuppence stopped dead in her tracks and turned to look at him.

'Jack!' she shrieked. 'Where on earth have you been?'

Jack didn't say anything. He just looked at her and grinned. Jack wasn't very confident about talking to people. He mostly got by with lots of nods and smiles.

'Maybe you just didn't notice him because he's so small?' said Jade.

All the other children laughed.

Miss Tuppence looked at her class and then at Jack. She was sure he hadn't been there a few minutes ago, but now he definitely was, and it looked for all the world as if he'd been sitting there the whole afternoon. She wondered if she was actually going mad.

'Well . . . how much have you written?' she asked.

Jack showed her his work. All he'd written was:

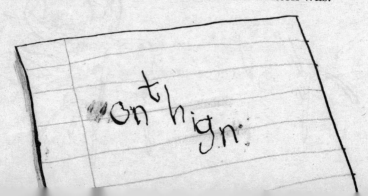

CHAPTER

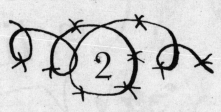

Jack's Aunt Violet was always too ill or too busy
to pick Jack up after school, so his spiteful cousin
Kelly picked him up instead. Cousin Kelly was a
lumpy teenager who was covered in spots. Her hair
was scraped up into a ponytail so tight that Jack
thought her face might split open at any moment.
She looked like an overripe tomato. With spots.

Cousin Kelly hated Jack and wasn't afraid to tell
him so.

'I hate you, I *hate* you, I **hate** you,'
she said, pulling her meanest face. Though Jack
thought there wasn't much difference between her
meanest face and her ordinary face.

You're ruining my life!

she screeched. 'If you weren't living with us and taking up all that space in the cupboard, my mum wouldn't have to keep the hoover in my room! It's all because your mum's a thief. I'm ashamed to walk down the street with you!'

They turned away from the school, but as soon as they were out of sight of the school gates Kelly shouted:

'Get lost! Scram!

I've got much more important things to do than babysit a little squirt like you all the way home!'

Jack knew what 'more important things' meant – sitting in the coffee shop with all her girlfriends, talking about hair and nails and clothes and pop stars, for hours and hours and hours. But he didn't mind walking home on his own because he never went straight home anyway. His favourite thing to do after school was visit Old Mr Mudge at his junkyard.

The junkyard was at the bottom of a little lane that led down to the canal. Jack thought the yard was a magical place. It was full of old fridges, washing machines and broken bikes. There was a big pile of chairs that had one leg missing, and a mountain of wardrobes that didn't have any doors. There were stacks of old tyres that Jack crawled in and out of, like tunnels, and in one corner of the yard lots of old cars were heaped on top of each other. Jack liked to get inside them and pretend he was driving.

But the most magical thing about the junkyard was the horses: Lightning the carthorse and Boadicea the Shetland pony.

Boadicea was an unusual name and Old Mr Mudge taught Jack how to say it properly: '*Bo* as in Bo-Peep, *D* as in the letter D, *sea* as in the North Sea, and *ugh* as in "ugh, you's trod in something nasty" – *Bo-D-sea-ugh*.'

He told Jack that it was the name of an ancient British queen – a fierce warrior who led an uprising against the Romans. Jack loved Boadicea, but he'd never seen anything look less like a fierce warrior queen than this short white pony.

Lightning might have been mistaken for a warrior king because he was so big and black that he almost blocked out the sun. His eyes were like goldfish bowls and his hooves were the size of giant frying pans.

But Boadicea only came up to Lightning's belly. In fact, she often walked right underneath.

No one could walk under Boadicea though – for

one thing, her legs were incredibly short, and, for
another, her belly was so fat that it almost brushed
the floor.

The two horses looked quite bizarre when they
stood side by side.

Old Mr Mudge used Lightning to pull the cart when he went out collecting junk, but he said Boadicea's job was just to keep Lightning company.

''Orses is like humans,' he said. 'They's needing a friend – otherwise they's going a bit crazy like.'

Old Mr Mudge was always pleased to see Jack, not just because Jack helped with the horses – he was very good at zipping up the ladder to the hayloft and pushing another bale down into the stable (which Old Mr Mudge found increasingly difficult) – but because he just liked having Jack around. They enjoyed the same things.

'We is like 'orses, ain't we, lad? We's be needing a friend too, otherwise we be going a bit crazy like. And we is friends cos we's liking the same things. We don't be needing any of that modern mumbo-jumbo. We don't be needing hairy planes and holidays in the Spanish river area. We just likes the simple life, and 'orses and such.'

Jack liked Old Mr Mudge and he liked working with the horses much more than being at school.

He even enjoyed 'mucking out' the stables, which meant sifting through the straw with a pitchfork and tossing all the horse poo into a bucket.

'That be good manure,' said Old Mr Mudge. 'Folks is paying a lot of money for a bag of that to put round their roses.'

You'd think that shovelling poo wouldn't be much fun, but Jack loved it. There was something very satisfying about making the stables clean and tidy, and once he'd done it he could get the horses in from the small field behind Old Mr Mudge's office and groom them.

Old Mr Mudge did Lightning, and Jack did Boadicea.

Boadicea loved being groomed. A big smile would spread across her face. She would close her eyes and lean hard into the brush. Quite often she squashed Jack against the stable door, and Jack would have to shout out, '*Oi!*'

Then she'd turn and look at him, and Jack sometimes thought she made a noise that sounded exactly like a human laugh.

After grooming came feeding.

Into their feed buckets Jack would tip some chopped carrots, some chaff – a mixture of barley straw cut into small pieces, with oil, mint and garlic – and then a couple of scoops of pony nuts.

Jack didn't know why they were called nuts, because they weren't nuts at all. They were made from a mixture of bran, oats, grass and molasses, and they looked more like pellets.

'Them pony nuts is like sweets to an 'orse,' said Old Mr Mudge. 'Best not be giving them too many, mind, especially Boadicea – only two scoops for her, on account of her not doing much work. Don't want to be giving her too much energy, otherwise there be no knowing what she might do.'

All the feed, apart from the hay, was kept in huge metal boxes, which were closed tight to stop the rats getting in and eating it all.

'Them's mighty popular with rats,' Old Mr Mudge would say, pointing at the pony nuts. 'Best keep the catches locked down.'

When Jack gave Boadicea her bucket of feed, she would often look at him with a hurt expression on her face. And she'd nod towards the metal bin with her head and then point to her feed bucket with her nose.

Everyone knows that horses can't talk, but sometimes Boadicea would flatten back her ears and make a noise somewhere between a neigh and a whinny that sounded exactly like, *Go on, put another scoop in.*

When Jack gave in and did as he was asked, her ears would relax and she would make a kind of snorting noise that sounded a bit like, *Thank you.* And once he thought she even winked at him.

Sometimes, after feeding, Old Mr Mudge would lift Jack up and sit him on Boadicea's back. Jack would grip with his knees and hold on to Boadicea's mane, and Old Mr Mudge would take hold of the lead rope and walk them up and down the towpath beside the canal. This was Jack's absolutely most favourite thing in the whole world.

Once he got overexcited and imagined he was a jockey in a very important horse race. He dug his heels into Boadicea's sides and slapped her bottom, like he'd seen them do on TV. Boadicea stopped immediately, and turned her head to look back at Jack with bulging eyes. Her tail swished violently

from side to side and the expression on her face seemed to say, *What on* earth *do you think you're doing? There's no call for that! I'll go in my own sweet time, thank you very much!*

'There be no need to hit the 'orse,' Old Mr Mudge said. ''Orses is like humans; they respond best to a bit of kindness. What us needs is some proper reins and a saddle, so as us don't fall off if her takes a mind to gallop. Minds you, you's not wanting to go too far along the canal or you's'll end up all the way across the country in Liverpool!'

After they'd finished working, they sat on two three-legged chairs that had been tied together to stop them falling over and drank huge mugs of tea. Old Mr Mudge liked talking to Jack. He knew the conversation was a bit one-sided, because Jack never said very much, but he also knew that Jack was listening, and Old Mr Mudge enjoyed the company.

'There be plenty of folks'd like to buy this yard

off me, what with it
being so near the
city centre and
all, but I don't
rightly see as I'd
like to change
at my age. I has
been here nigh

on eighty years, and my dad
afore me and his dad afore him. I likes it here. And
the 'orses likes it here. And you likes it here too,
don't you, Jack my lad? You's got a feeling for the
junk, I knows it. Junkyard Jack – that's you.'

Jack smiled and nodded in agreement. He liked
being called Junkyard Jack, and he wished that he
could live at the yard with Lightning, Boadicea and
Old Mr Mudge.

He remembered his mum telling him stories

about when she and Aunt Violet were younger. They used to live on a farm with cows and sheep and horses. She told him how wonderful it had been, how they used to ride every day and how much they'd loved their horses. But something went wrong, and they had to sell the farm and move into the city, and that's when Jack was born and his mum had to get a job working in a hotel.

The clock in Old Mr Mudge's office chimed six o'clock.

'It be time you scootled off home now, young 'un,' said Old Mr Mudge. 'Or your auntie'll be a-wondering where you be.'

CHAPTER

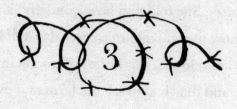

Ever since his mum had gone to prison, Jack had been living with Aunt Violet and her family. They lived on the top floor of a very tall block of flats.

Aunt Violet was an extraordinarily timid woman, and everything about her was grey: her hair was grey, her clothes were grey, her skin was grey; even her teeth were grey. And she was always ill. She was forever sniffing and snuffling and sneezing.

Aunt Violet was married to Uncle Ted. He was a grumpy, bad-tempered man who spent most of the day shouting at the TV. He was also very fat because he ate buckets of popcorn all day long. And the popcorn had a very bad effect on his bowels. When Uncle Ted walked around, he let out a bit of wind with every step – it sounded like someone was playing the tuba.

Oompah-popperty-pumperty-pump parp!

he went as he waddled along.

Although he didn't waddle about very often. In fact, the only time he got out of his armchair was to go to watch a football match every Saturday.

Jack never went into the sitting room when Uncle Ted was there, firstly because of the pong and secondly because Uncle Ted shouted horrible things at him:

'We never wanted you here in the first place! You're a terrible burden and no mistake!'

parp.

'Your thieving mum is lucky she's in prison – at least she doesn't have to see *you* every day!'

Guff.

'Why doesn't your dad look after you? That Joe Sampson – what a waste of space he was. He's rolling in money, but does he ever send us a penny to help raise his son? No, he doesn't.'

Honk.

Aunt Violet would sometimes try and speak up for Jack, saying it wasn't his fault that his parents had split up or that his mum was in prison, but this just seemed to make Uncle Ted even angrier. Which made Uncle Ted's flatulence even worse – when he got really angry, it sounded like an entire brass band had lost their way while playing the chorus of 'Land of Hope and Glory'.

So Jack spent most of his time in his bedroom. Although, as you already know, it wasn't a bedroom; it was just a big cupboard. It was the sort of cupboard that some people might call 'the box room' or 'the airing cupboard' – the place where they kept the boiler.

It didn't have a window and was very cramped. It wasn't even big enough for a regular mattress, so Jack slept on an old cot mattress that lay on top of the suitcase that held all his belongings.

Every shelf was taken up with boxes full of football programmes.

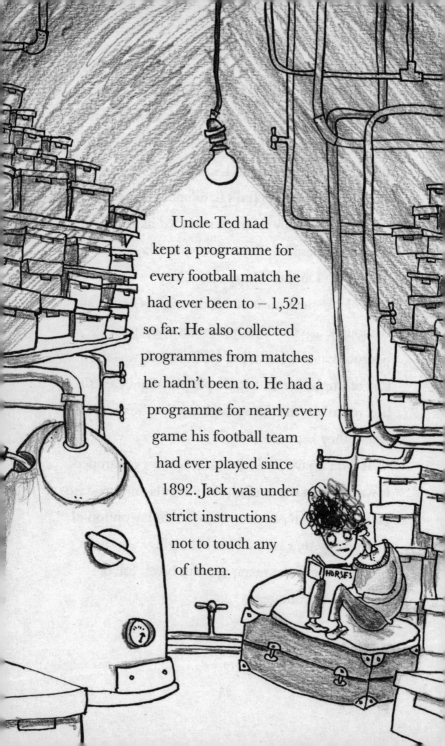

Uncle Ted had kept a programme for every football match he had ever been to – 1,521 so far. He also collected programmes from matches he hadn't been to. He had a programme for nearly every game his football team had ever played since 1892. Jack was under strict instructions not to touch any of them.

'If you do, you'll be sorry!' his uncle had yelled at him, letting one rip, like a bugler sounding reveille. 'That collection's worth thousands of pounds! There's some in the box on the top shelf that would fetch five hundred quid on their own!

So hands off!'

A single bare light bulb hung from a cord in the middle of the cupboard, but the switch for it was out in the corridor, and whenever Kelly walked past she would flick it off, even if she knew Jack was in there.

He only had one book, but he really liked it. It was a book about horses. There were some words in it, but it was mostly pictures. It showed all the different breeds of horse and their colourings, every sort of bit, bridle and saddle, and lots more. His mum used to read it to him when he was younger and he knew everything off by heart.

He liked to sit on his mattress and go through the whole book, pointing and naming everything he saw: Exmoor pony, Welsh mountain pony, Icelandic trotting pony; Appaloosa, skewbald, palomino; western bridle, snaffle bridle, double bridle . . . There were so many things to name in the book that it took Jack over an hour to get through them all. Even when Kelly turned out the light, he didn't complain: he just carried on reading by the light of the flame from the boiler.

Jack's only friends in the flat were some mice that lived behind the skirting board. When Jack heard Old Mr Mudge say that rats liked pony nuts, he imagined that mice might like them too. So he always brought a few home with him, and he would lay them on the floor and then sit back and watch.

After a minute or so, the mice would come out

from the shadows. The one at the front would look at the pony nuts and then up at Jack. Jack would nod and say, 'Help yourself.'

Then the lead mouse would seem to signal to the others that it was safe, and they would all run out and nibble away until there was nothing left.

Jack loved to watch them, especially the one that didn't so much eat as stuff everything into her cheeks.

Once they'd finished, the mice would scurry away, but the lead mouse would look back at Jack and nod, as if he was saying thank you.

'You're very welcome,' Jack would say. 'I'll try and bring some more tomorrow.'

And the mouse would politely nod again before disappearing behind the skirting board.

The only other room where Jack felt safe was the bathroom because he could go in there and lock the door. Quite often he went in there even if he didn't need the loo. He would pull up the blind and look out of the window. They were so high up it was like being in an aeroplane.

He could see the town square down below, and all the people hurrying about like an army of ants. The whole town was spread out before him, and beyond the town he could see the countryside. And even further away in the distance he could see two hills separated by a dark wood.

On top of one hill was a grand hotel. He knew that this was the Courtly Manor Hotel where his mum had once worked.

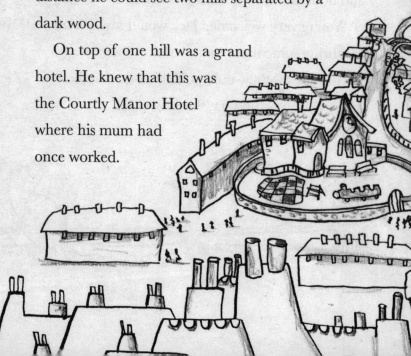

And on the opposite hill stood a prison behind giant walls covered in coils of barbed wire. That was where his mum lived now.

He liked to look at the prison and open the little locket and look at the photo of his mum. The locket had space for two photos. Jack would have liked to put a photo of his dad on the other side, but he'd never met him because his parents had split up before he was born, so he didn't have one.

His mum didn't like talking about Jack's dad, but Jack knew he was called Joe Sampson, so he'd written *Joe Sampson* as carefully as he could on a scrap of paper and put it on the empty side of the locket. Well, Jack thought it said *Joe Sampson*, but what he'd actually written was:

Jeo SamspOOn

He closed the locket and looked down to the left, where he could see his school, and then he followed the little lane down to the canal, where he could see the junkyard. If he looked really carefully, he could spot Lightning and Boadicea in the field behind the office. He couldn't see them very well, but he could definitely tell that it was them – Lightning was so big and black and Boadicea so small and white.

Sometimes when he looked he couldn't see them because they were in the stable. The first time this happened he stared at the stable, willing them to come out, and after about ten minutes, lo and behold, they did! And the funny thing was that, once they were out, they turned and looked at Jack's block of flats. He couldn't quite see their eyes, but they were definitely facing in his direction, with their heads tilted up.

So he practised staring at the stable and thinking very hard about them, and willing them to come out and look at him, and now, whenever he went to the window, he could get them to come out of the stable in less than a minute, and often straight away. In fact, sometimes they seemed to have come out just before he got to the window and were already standing there, waiting for him.

Jack wondered if he actually had special powers where the horses were concerned. But, whether he did or not, when they turned to look at him, he felt very close to them.

CHAPTER

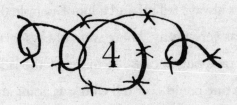

Jack's favourite day of the week was Saturday, for three reasons. One: he didn't have to go to school, which meant that he didn't have to do any reading or writing. Two: his uncle went to a football match, which meant that Jack could go into the sitting room. And three: the horse racing was on TV.

Jack loved horse racing. He'd loved it ever since he was a baby. His mum soon learned that the only thing guaranteed to stop him crying – when he'd been teething or when he'd fallen over and hurt himself – was to put the horse racing on the TV. He would sit and watch it for hours.

Jack's favourite race was called the Grand National. It happened once a year and it was the most famous race in the world. It was popular because the jumps were so big that some of the jockeys always fell off and a lot of people thought this was very funny. There were always forty horses in the race but, because so many of the riders fell off, no one could ever tell who was going to win, which made it exciting to watch.

Jack had always wanted to be a jockey. When he was a toddler, he used to get his mum to crawl around the room while he sat on her back, shouting,

'Giddy-up!'

His mum grew tired of this, so on his third birthday she bought him a rocking horse. He loved it, and rode it for hours on end, rocking back and forth, pretending to be in a race.

When his mum went to prison and he moved in with Aunt Violet, Uncle Ted said they didn't have enough room for the rocking horse, so it had to be sold.

Jack had tried to make other things in the flat into a horse. He'd tried sitting on the radiator, but that burned his bottom.

He tried sitting on the edge of the bath, but it was so slippery he kept falling off.

And he'd even tried the ironing board, but that had a nasty habit of collapsing whenever he started to gallop.

The best place by far was the arm of Uncle Ted's chair. It was exactly the right width and

height, and Jack
made a set of reins
out of string, which
he could loop round the
end of the armchair
to make it more
realistic.

On this Saturday Jack was just attaching the reins
to the chair when his horrible cousin Kelly slobbed
into the sitting room.

'What are you doing, you pathetic twerp?' she
shouted. 'You haven't got time for your stupid
pretend horse racing today because you've got to
go to prison! To visit your mum, the thief.'

Jack had forgotten it was visiting day. Every
fourth Saturday Aunt Violet would take him to visit
his mum. He was happy it was visiting day because
he really wanted to see his mum, but he wished
visiting day was on a weekday. If it was, he'd have

a day off school. And he wouldn't miss the racing . . .

To make things worse, Kelly sang a horrible song she'd made up about Jack's mum. She'd changed the words to a skipping song, and it went like this:

Not last night but the night before

Stupid Jack's mum came **robbing** *at my door.*

She **stole** *my watch and she* **stole** *my ring*

But I knocked her on the head with a **rolling pin**.

Jack's mum's a **swindler**, *Jack's mum's a* **cheat**,

Jack's mum's a **criminal**, a robber *and* **a thief**.

Lock her in a **DUNGEON** *full of* slimy snails –

Stupid Jack's mum must **GO TO JAIL!**

'Now, now, there's no need for that,' said Aunt Violet, popping her head round the door.

'But she is a thief, Mum,' said Kelly. 'She's a kleptomaniac – that's what the judge said.'

'The judge said nothing of the sort,' said Aunt Violet. 'And poor Bridget has no idea how the necklace ended up in her bag. Someone put it in there without her knowing.'

'Oh, pull the other one,' sneered Kelly.

'Come on, Jack – you'd better get your coat on or we'll miss the bus,' said Aunt Violet. 'What are you up to today, Kelly?'

'Oh, me and the girls are going to the new nail bar on the high street – I'm having a full gel nail polish and manicure.'

'I don't know where you get the money from,' said Aunt Violet. 'I work all the hours God sends and there's still nothing left at the end of the week.'

'I'm using my birthday money.'

'I don't know how you've still got any left – it's six months since your birthday,' said Aunt Violet, and she tied her headscarf round her head and led Jack out of the flat, closing the door behind them.

As soon as they were gone, Kelly ran down the corridor and went into Jack's cupboard. She reached up to one of the boxes on the top shelf and pulled out a football programme.

'*At home to Sheffield Wednesday, February 1923,*' she read. 'Yes, that should be worth a few quid. Thanks, Dad, you moron.'

But then she suddenly froze, for there, on the shelf, level with her face and looking straight at her, was a little mouse.

'*Arghhh!*'

screamed Kelly, too frightened to move.

The mouse stared at her. If you'd been there, you might have thought the mouse raised an eyebrow, as if to say, *And what do you think you're doing, young lady?* But how could that be? Mice don't have eyebrows.

The mouse seemed to shake its head in bitter disappointment as Kelly slowly backed out of the cupboard and slammed the door shut.

'Stupid Jack – he must have been eating cheese in there!' she grumbled, stuffing the programme into her handbag and running out of the flat.

CHAPTER

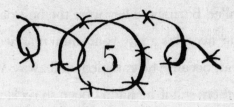

Jack always enjoyed the bus journey to the prison, not just because he was looking forward to seeing his mum, but because the bus went past the farm where his mum and Aunt Violet used to live when they were girls.

It was called Broadacre Farm, and Jack knew exactly where it was. He knew that, after they drove through a little village with a duck pond in front of the church, the farm was only two bends of the road away.

Aunt Violet had pointed it out the first time they'd visited the prison.

'That's Broadacre Farm,' she'd said. 'That's where your mum and I grew up. Oh, it was so lovely. It was a proper farm. We had cows and

sheep and pigs and ponies, and even a donkey
called Barnaby. They were the best days of
our lives. It's a pity your mum married your
dad, because he gambled it all away. We'd be
there still if he hadn't been so reckless.'

The bus passed the church with the duck pond
in front, and Jack edged forward in his seat. One
bend, two bends, and there it was. It was such a cosy
little farm, with red-and-white checked curtains in
the windows, daffodils in window boxes and a lovely
front porch stacked with logs for the fire.

To the side of the house there was a lovely yard
with stables for horses, but all the stables were
empty.

Aunt Violet was busy reading the instructions on a bottle of flu medicine. When Jack nudged her with his elbow, she looked up and he pointed to the farm.

She broke into a sad grey smile when she saw it, and then an expression of surprise slowly spread over her face.

45

'Well, look at that,' she said, pointing to a big noticeboard by the side of the road. 'It's up for sale!'

Jack tried to read the big noticeboard, but the letters wouldn't stay still. It said something like **O**^{RF} **L**A_SE or **F**^{RO} **S**A_EL.

'Well, I never,' his aunt continued. 'Who would have thought it? Up for sale. Whoever gets it has to be the luckiest person in the world.'

As soon as Jack's mum came into the visiting room at the prison, she ran over to Jack and picked him up and squeezed him tight.

'Oh, Jack, how I've missed you! Oh, I love you so much! I've been aching to see you!' she cried, spinning him round and round and laughing through her tears.

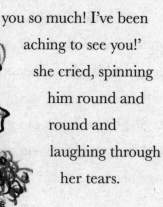

Jack could never think what to say, but he was beaming the biggest smile in the world.

'Let me look at you,' she said, leaning back to get a better view. 'I'd like to say how much you've grown, but you haven't really, have you?'

Jack smiled and shook his head.

'You're just the same lovely Jack you've always been, my little angel,' continued his mother.

'Bridget, you'll never guess,' said Aunt Violet, 'but Broadacre Farm is up for sale. We saw the notice-board as we came past on the bus, didn't we, Jack?'

Jack nodded.

'First time it's come up for sale since that no-good Joe Sampson gambled it all away,' Aunt Violet carried on.

'Oh, please let's not get into that again, Vi,' said Jack's mum. 'That's all in the past now and there's nothing we can do about it.'

They had cups of tea, and biscuits, and after the initial excitement of the visit had subsided Jack's mum got round to talking about the thing she always talked about during these visits – the fact that she was innocent and that Mrs Scrimshank had got off scot-free.

Jack knew the story off by heart:

It had all happened on the first of April – April Fool's Day – which had made his mum think it was a joke to begin with, but it had turned into a horrible nightmare.

Mrs Scrimshank was the owner of the Courtly Manor Hotel. She was a mean old lady with a face like a shrivelled-up prune, who was famously unkind to everyone who worked for her.

One day, while Jack's mum was working there as a chambermaid, she walked into one of the hotel bedrooms to clean and tidy it, and found Mrs Scrimshank in there, which was odd, because Mrs Scrimshank didn't normally visit the bedrooms.

Mrs Scrimshank looked a bit flustered and surprised.

'Just checking there were enough towels in the bathroom,' she said.

But Jack's mum saw that she was hiding something shiny in her hand and thought it was rather strange. And later the guest whose room it was – a posh woman called Lady Davenport – complained that a diamond necklace had gone missing from her bedside drawer!

The police were called and Jack's mum told them that she'd seen Mrs Scrimshank leaving the room with something shiny in her hands.

Mrs Scrimshank pretended to be horrified and said she'd never been anywhere near the room.

She said there were security cameras all over the hotel that recorded to a machine in her office and that the recording would prove her right.

They all went into her office to look, but discovered that the disk in the machine had gone missing.

'Whoever stole the necklace probably got rid of the disk,' said Mrs Scrimshank. 'I suggest you search the staff locker room.'

The police did and, although they didn't find the disk, they found the diamond necklace in Jack's mum's bag!

And she was charged with theft and sent to prison.

'But I'm sure the disk is

still there,' said Jack's mum. 'And it will prove that I'm innocent.'

'Oh, Bridget,' said Aunt Violet. 'We've been through this before. The police searched high and low and couldn't find it. They searched the bins – they even raked through the ash in the fireplace – but they couldn't find a trace.'

'There's a new girl sharing my cell,' said Jack's mum. 'She's heard rumours about Mrs Scrimshank. They say that she's stolen lots of things from the guests and that she hides them in a secret room underneath her office. You have to tell the police!'

'But the case is closed, Bridget, and you've only got another year to go.'

'I can't spend another year in this place, Vi – seeing Jack for just an hour, once a month. You have to get the police to reopen the case. Or, better still, go to the hotel and find the secret room.'

'Oh, don't ask me to do that, Bridget! I can't go snooping around the hotel – I'd get arrested and end up in here with you.'

'But it's my reputation!' said Jack's mum. 'I'm not a thief, and I won't have people saying I am when I'm not.'

CHAPTER

When Jack and Aunt Violet got back to the flat, Kelly ran out of her room to meet them. She had a dangerous grin on her face and her eyes were brimming with spiteful pleasure.

'You'll never guess what happened today,' she said, looking ever so pleased with her news. 'Oh, there was such a lot of blood. It looked like a giant had emptied an enormous bottle of tomato ketchup all over the high street.'

'What is it? What's happened?' asked Aunt Violet.

'You know that smelly old guy who Jack goes to visit? The one with the horse and cart? Well, he's only had a head-on crash with a huge lorry!

Yeah, just there in the high street – it smashed right into them. The horse looked in a really bad way, and they took the old man off to the hospital in an ambulance,' she said, leaning down and laughing right in Jack's face, 'but I bet he doesn't make it.'

Jack couldn't believe what he was hearing.

Old Mr Mudge! And Lightning!

Without even thinking, he began to run.

'Jack, where are you going?' asked Aunt Violet.

But Jack didn't reply. He just ran out of the flat, slamming the door behind him. Aunt Violet couldn't possibly go after him – she was far too unwell. And Kelly was still laughing.

'Don't you be long!' Aunt Violet shouted. 'It's getting late already!'

Jack didn't think even horrible Kelly could have made up a story like that, but his first thought was to run to the junkyard and check if it was true.

He couldn't tell whether he was about to cry or whether his eyes were watering from running so fast into the wind.

When he reached the junkyard, he saw a white van with its doors open. Two workmen were fixing a big sign to the junkyard gates. Jack tried to read it, but the words kept getting jumbled up. It said something like:

CLODES. PEEK TOU- GANDER.

The workmen had already put an enormous lock and chain round the gates. Jack stood and stared, but he didn't know what to do. He didn't know what was happening, except that if the gates were locked he wouldn't be able to get in.

'What is it, kid? What d'you want?' asked one of the workmen.

Jack wanted to say, 'Where's Old Mr Mudge and the horses?' But the words wouldn't come out and he just stood there, staring, with tears pricking at his eyes.

'Can't you read the sign, kid?' said the man. '*Closed. Keep out. Danger.*'

The two men finished fixing the sign and began to put their tools back in the van. Jack went over to the gates and gently pushed against them to see if they really *were* locked tight. They were.

'If you're looking for the old man and his horse, they're not here any more, kid,' said the first workman. 'Haven't you heard? There was an accident. The old man's in hospital, but it looked very serious. And I don't think the horse survived.'

Jack turned and looked at him. With an enormous effort, he managed to say in a small, thin voice, 'But what about Boadicea?'

'Boad-a-what?'

'B-Boadicea,' stammered Jack. 'The Shetland pony. She's in there.'

'Listen, kid,' said the man. 'There's nothing left in there except a big pile of junk. Now clear off out of it!'

The men finished loading the van and drove away.

Jack tried again to pull the gates open, but they

were made of metal and the lock was very strong.
He called out for Boadicea.

Boadicea!
Boadicea!

He listened hard for any kind of a reply, but he couldn't hear one.

Not a single whinny.

Not a snort.

Not a nicker.

Perhaps the men were right – perhaps she wasn't there. There was only one way to find out for sure, thought Jack, and that was to ask Old Mr Mudge.

Jack remembered where the hospital was because he'd often seen it when he was looking down from the bathroom window. He knew it was the big white building near the city centre.

No matter where he was, he could always see the block of flats he lived in, so by looking up at them, he could see his bathroom window and imagine himself looking down at the hospital. That way he could work out where to go.

CHAPTER

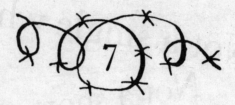

It was a big, busy hospital.

Jack wasn't sure that he should be there on his own, so he sneaked round corners, hid behind trolleys and pillars and tiptoed along the sides of corridors. None of the doctors and nurses noticed him.

He had no idea where Old Mr Mudge might be. There were lots of signs in the corridors that said things like X-YAR and EGERMENCIES, and a very confusing one that said GYNAECOLOGY.

He crept from room to room, keeping to the shadows.

He searched everywhere, and eventually found a ward full of old people. He ghosted around the room, checking every bed, and in the very last one he found Old Mr Mudge.

Old Mr Mudge had a bandage round his head, and tubes going into his arm. There was a curly wire that connected him to a machine that kept going

beep . . .

beep . . .

beep.

His eyes were closed and he was breathing very slowly. Jack's class had visited a blacksmith as part of their project about the Industrial Revolution, and Old Mr Mudge's breathing sounded like the enormous bellows the blacksmith had used to make the fire glow red.

Jack crept up to the side of the bed. He didn't want to disturb Old Mr Mudge and he didn't know what to say or how to say it. But he wanted him to wake up, so he blew gently on Old Mr Mudge's face. The old man's face twitched. He looked like a sleeping dog having a dream about rabbits. But he didn't wake up.

Jack blew a bit harder. Old Mr Mudge's face twitched a little more, and then one of his eyes opened. At first he looked confused, but then an enormous smile slowly spread across his face.

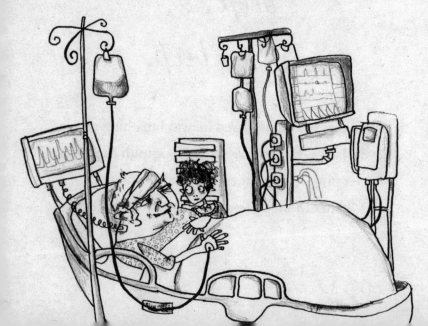

'Young Jack,' he said. 'You's come to see me in hospital, have you? That be right nice of you, young 'un. I's afraid I's in a bit of a bad way.'

Jack's face showed a curious mixture of joy at having found Old Mr Mudge and fear of how serious his injuries might be. Old Mr Mudge seemed to be able to read Jack's mind.

'You's heard about the accident, young 'un?'

Jack nodded his head.

'I's afraid 'tis true, young 'un. It were an awful accident. Them lorries pays no attention to 'orses these days. They's not looking where they be going.'

Struggling to speak, Jack finally said, 'Lightning?'

'I's afraid he is no more, God bless his soul.'

Jack fought to hold back his tears, then managed to say, 'And what about Boadicea?'

'I don't rightly know, young 'un,' said Old Mr Mudge. 'They's told me they's be taking care of her, but I don't knows where she be to. I expects she be in some kind of 'orse sanctuary or the like.'

Jack understood that this was probably the best thing for Boadicea, but he was instantly heartbroken at the thought of never seeing her again.

Old Mr Mudge watched Jack's brow furrowing as the boy processed his thoughts. 'As soon as I is better, I's going to get her back and you can see her as much as you like,' he said. 'After all, you's looking after her so much she be practically your pony, anyways.'

Jack smiled at the thought that Boadicea was practically his.

'You know, young Jack,' said Old Mr Mudge, fixing Jack with the kindest smile, 'I ain't never had no son, nor no grandson or the like, but you be the closest thing to family I's ever had . . .'

He looked like he wanted to carry on talking, but something seemed to switch off inside him. His head sank deep into his pillow and his eyes closed.

The machine made an alarming sound and two nurses rushed towards the bed.

Jack didn't want to get into trouble, so he quickly slipped away. He reached the end of the ward and turned to see what was happening. The nurses were working on Old Mr Mudge. They took his pulse, checked his eyes with a torch and looked at the machine. One of them quickly gave him an injection, but the machine kept making the same alarming noise. After a while the two nurses gave each other a look and shook their heads, and Jack knew that Old Mr Mudge was dead.

CHAPTER

Jack traipsed all the way home, feeling sadder than he'd ever felt in his entire life. His mum was in prison, Old Mr Mudge had died, so had Lightning, and he had no idea where Boadicea was, but he knew he'd never see her again.

To make things worse, he had to live at Aunt Violet's with horrible Uncle Ted and his vile cousin Kelly.

When he got back to the flat, his aunt poked her head round the kitchen door. She smiled at Jack sympathetically because she knew that he was fond of Old Mr Mudge and the horses and that he might be upset.

'You're just in time for tea. I've made your

favourite – chicken nuggets with oven chips,' she said.

Chicken nuggets with oven chips wasn't Jack's favourite, but it was all his aunt could make. They had chicken nuggets with oven chips every day, at every meal. It all looked horrible, as usual. The chips were burnt on one side and white and uncooked on the other. The chicken nuggets were grey and soggy.

'I'm not hungry,' said Jack very quietly.

'That's all right, dear. I understand,' said Aunt Violet, picking up the plate and getting ready to scrape the food into the bin.

There was the sound of a huge trombone, and Jack turned to see Uncle Ted standing in the kitchen door.

'What's going on here?' he said.

'The poor lad's a bit upset,' said Aunt Violet. 'He's off his food.'

'He'll eat it and be thankful – put it back on the table,' barked Uncle Ted.

Aunt Violet was too timid to refuse, so she put the plate back down. Uncle Ted waddled into the kitchen –

Oompah-Poompah-parperty-parp.

He pulled back a kitchen chair and signalled for Jack to sit on it. With a heavy heart, Jack did as he was told and sat there with the disgusting nuggets and oven chips right under his nose. The nuggets smelled horrible – even worse than Uncle Ted's farts.

'Now listen to me,' said Uncle Ted, sitting down on the chair opposite, to the sound of a dying bugle. 'We've welcomed you into our home. We've made huge sacrifices for you. We've worked our fingers to the bone to put good food on the table for you . . .

AND YOU ARE GOING TO EAT IT!!!'

His anger brought on an attack of flatulence that sounded like a euphonium exploding. Kelly heard the noise and came from her bedroom to watch the fun. There was nothing she liked better than watching someone get bullied.

'Don't be too hard on him, Ted. He's had some bad news,' said Aunt Violet.

'Leave it out, Violet! I'm the boss in this house! Now EAT!' he shouted, stabbing a chicken nugget with a fork and holding it right in front of Jack's mouth.

Jack couldn't believe what his life had become. He couldn't see what fun there was to be had: no Mum, no horses, no Mudge. Just school, and letters jumping about, and Cousin Kelly and Uncle Ted, and chicken nuggets with oven chips.

'No,' he said. But he said it so quietly that no one could hear what he'd said.

'What was that?' said Uncle Ted, slowly leaning forward to the thin, high-pitched squeak of a cornet playing top C.

'I said *no*,' said Jack, clearly and precisely.

'Wow – it talks!' laughed Kelly.

'You'll do as I say!'

shouted Uncle Ted, lunging forward to grab Jack, to a chorus of French horns.

But Jack slipped quickly out of his

chair, darted under the table and made a dash
for the door. He scampered between Kelly's
legs, bolted down the corridor and ran into the
bathroom, slamming the door shut behind him and
quickly turning the key in the lock.

Uncle Ted came along the corridor, grabbing the
handle and rattling it up and down.

'He's locked it! He's blummin' well
locked it!'

'Oh, Ted, don't be too hard on him.
He's Bridget's boy – our flesh and
blood,' said Aunt Violet timidly.

'He's *your* flesh and blood,
not mine,' said Uncle Ted.

'He's not proper family, is he, Dad?' piped up Kelly. 'And he's horrible and ungrateful. Why don't we stick him in an orphanage? Then I wouldn't have to keep the hoover in my room.'

'Good idea, Kelly love. First thing Monday morning I'm going to ring the authorities and get him taken away, the ungrateful brat,' said Uncle Ted, banging on the door and trying to force it. But, no matter what he did, it wouldn't open.

Jack stayed quiet. He couldn't be bothered to argue. He didn't know how he was going to get out of the trouble he was in, but he knew he wouldn't give in just yet.

'He's got to come out some time or he'll starve to death – we'll just have to wait,' said Uncle Ted, giving the handle another good rattling.

Jack could hear them standing there on the other side of the door, but they got bored pretty quickly.

'I'm going to watch a bit of telly and eat some popcorn while we're waiting,' said Uncle Ted, and Jack heard him waddle back to the sitting room with a *rumperty-pumperty-parp* that got quieter as he went further away.

'You'd better not touch any of my stuff in there!' shouted Kelly through the keyhole, before she too flounced off back to her room. Jack looked at all her beauty products on the shelves. There must have been thirty bottles of lotions and potions. He wondered how she could still be so ugly when she had all that.

Aunt Violet tapped gently on the door.

'Open the door, Jack, there's a good lad,' she whispered. 'Just say sorry to your uncle and eat your nuggets and everything will be fine.'

But Jack didn't make a sound, and after a while even Aunt Violet went back to the kitchen.

Jack stayed in the bathroom all evening.

Uncle Ted got so desperate to use the loo that he actually did a wee in the teapot.

'Oh, Ted, I'll never drink tea again,' moaned Aunt Violet. Even Kelly thought it was pretty gross.

Before they went to bed the three of them had to wash their faces in the kitchen sink with washing-up liquid and clean their teeth by rubbing salt on to them with their fingers.

But eventually they all went to bed.

Jack couldn't think of going to sleep, even though the bath looked bigger than his cot mattress. He pulled

up the window blind and peered
out. The town looked very
different at night. The moon was
just emerging from behind a cloud.
It illuminated the canal, which sparkled like a silk
ribbon, and it shone down on the old junkyard.
Jack could see reflections from the mirrors on some
of the wrecked cars.

Then Jack's heart suddenly skipped a beat.
What was that he could see? He rubbed his
eyes and looked again to make sure. Yes, in the
small field at the back of the junkyard – the field
behind Old Mr Mudge's office – there was a white
shape glowing in the moonlight. It had four short
legs, a head and a tail . . . It was Boadicea! Jack
didn't know whether the moonlight had special
magnifying powers, but he could make her out
much more clearly than usual. He thought he
could see her eyes, and she was definitely looking
straight back at him!

CHAPTER

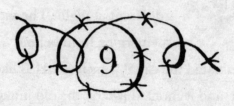

9

Jack slipped out of the bathroom as quietly as one of his mouse friends. He was clever enough to take the key and lock the bathroom door from the outside, so that everyone would think he was still in there, then he crept noiselessly out of the flat, squeezing the front door shut behind him.

In no time at all he was at the junkyard gates. The lock and chain the workmen had put on were still there, so Jack went round to the side entrance – the small gate that led on to the canal towpath.

This gate was locked too, but Jack remembered a time when Lightning had bashed into it on his way through and damaged the lower hinge. Pushing with all his might at the bottom of the gate, he managed to make an opening just big enough to slip through – and he was in!

He ran through the yard to the field behind Old Mr Mudge's office, and there was Boadicea! She had a look on her face that said, *About time too.*

Jack rushed over to throw his arms round her, but Boadicea barged right past him and trotted quickly towards the stable. She turned to Jack as she went, beckoning him with her head, as if to say, *This way, you idiot.*

Boadicea trotted straight up to the massive feed bin where Old Mr Mudge kept the pony nuts. Then she did something Jack had never seen her do before – she lifted one leg and tapped the top of the big metal box.

Jack watched in astonishment. She nodded her head and pushed her feed bucket towards him.

Jack was amazed. Of course! She hadn't been fed since the morning. But he couldn't believe what he'd just seen. He was almost in a trance as he undid the catch on the box and poured two scoopfuls into Boadicea's feed bucket.

Boadicea looked at them, then glared back at Jack and rolled her eyes. Jack thought he even heard her sigh. Then she kicked the big metal box and shoved the feed bucket back towards him.

Jack smiled. He got another scoopful of pony nuts and poured them into her bucket.

Boadicea stuck her head in and, with her nose, dragged the bucket away from Jack so that she could eat in peace.

There was something about being with horses that made it easier for Jack to speak. Jack didn't know what it was. Maybe it was because he knew that they couldn't talk back or really understand what he was saying, so they wouldn't judge him.

'What a cheeky little pony,' said Jack, closing the lid to the big metal box.

'Oh, shut up,' said Boadicea.

Or at least that's what Jack thought she said. But who'd ever heard of a talking horse? There was a noise that Old Mr Mudge called 'nickering'; a sort of rumbling sound that horses made in their throats. Jack wondered whether that was what he'd heard. But it had definitely sounded like, 'Oh, shut up.'

'Did you just say, "Oh, shut up"?' asked Jack.

Boadicea froze. Slowly she lifted her head and gazed over her shoulder at him. They looked each other in the eye.

'Did you just say, "Oh, shut up"?' repeated Jack. 'Did you just talk?'

Boadicea seemed to think very carefully for a minute, then, in a very deliberate way, she neighed. Though Jack thought she hadn't neighed the way she usually did; it was more like she'd actually said the word *neigh*.

But whatever she'd said or hadn't said, Boadicea seemed to think that this was the end of the matter and she turned back to her feed bucket.

Jack shook his head and decided he'd been mistaken. He was quite tired – it was very late – so he must have misheard.

After all the bad news, it was so lovely being at the yard with Boadicea. The gates were locked so no one could get in and nobody knew he was there. He could do what he liked. Everyone thought he was locked in the bathroom. He could stay all night.

Jack didn't have any food, but then he remembered there were lots of carrots in the other feed bin, and he lifted the lid and helped himself to one.

Boadicea turned round and gave him a hard stare.

'Oh, sorry, Boadicea, do you want a carrot too?' said Jack.

Boadicea nodded her head.

Jack looked at her. 'Can you actually understand what I'm saying?' he said.

Boadicea pulled a rather worried-looking face, as if she was trying to get a bit of pony nut out from between her teeth with her tongue.

Jack grabbed a handful of carrots and fed them to her one by one, stroking her forehead at the same time. She responded by gently pushing her neck into him, and Jack put an arm round it and hugged her.

'You're my favourite thing in the whole wide world,' he said.

Boadicea stopped munching and looked at him, then flicked her head towards him. If you'd been there, you might have thought that she actually gave Jack a little kiss on the cheek.

And then she went back to her food.

Jack mooched about the yard and tidied things up a bit. He mucked out the stable and filled up Boadicea's water bucket. Then he groomed her to get any bits of mud off her coat.

He didn't know what time it was exactly, but he thought it must be the middle of the night. He decided he ought to get some sleep. He tried Old Mr Mudge's office, but the door was locked. Then he saw the ladder to the hayloft and had a brainwave.

The hayloft, he said to himself. *Oh, it'd be nice and comfy in there.*

Wearily he climbed the ladder and pushed some of the loose hay around to make himself a kind of nest. He loved the smell of hay anyway, and it was so soft and welcoming. He lay down and, in approximately one second flat, he was fast asleep.

CHAPTER

'Jack,' came a loud whisper.

Jack stirred in his sleep.

'Jack,' came the loud whisper again.

Jack opened his eyes and sat up. Someone was whispering his name, but he didn't recognize the voice.

'Jack!' came the whisper again, even louder than before.

Jack inched towards the edge of the hayloft and cautiously peeked down into the stable below. Boadicea was staring right back at him.

'Great heavens, there you are at last,' she said, rather annoyed. 'Those workmen in the white van have come back. I don't know what they want, but

I don't like the look of them.'

'You can talk!' said Jack, utterly astonished.

'Shh! Shh!

Keep your voice down or they'll hear you.'

'But you can talk,' said Jack, less loudly but no less astonished.

'Well . . . yes, I can talk,' said Boadicea, rather begrudgingly. 'Hoorah and fiddlesticks,' she added, somewhat sarcastically.

'But that's incredible,' said Jack, as he swiftly lowered himself on to the ladder and scuttled down to the bottom.

'Yes, it is. I am obviously an incredible horse,' she said in a resigned, matter-of-fact sort of way. 'But can we just drop the "Yikes! Isn't that amazing!" nonsense for a minute. I'm in serious trouble here! When they were here yesterday, they were talking about carting me off to the knacker's yard when they found me.'

'What's the knacker's yard?' asked Jack.

'It's the place where they . . .' Boadicea was reluctant to say it. 'It's the place where they kill old horses that aren't any use to anyone any more.'

'That's horrible!'

'Yes, I tend to agree with you,' she said. 'So we must get on! Yesterday, when they came, I hid behind Old Mudge's outside toilet, but this time they seem to be making a more thorough search of the place. I've got to get out of here sharpish and I need your help.'

'But what can I do?' asked Jack, still completely flabbergasted to see Boadicea's mouth working and human words coming out.

'There's a key to the gate that leads on to the canal. It's hanging up there behind the feed bin. You may have noticed that I've only got hooves, so fiddly keys are a bit beyond me. I need you to unlock the gate so I can skedaddle.'

'Of course!' said Jack, who'd never heard the word *skedaddle* before, but assumed that it meant 'run away'.

'There it is – look,' said Boadicea, pointing with a hoof to the key, which was on a hook behind the feed bin. Jack grabbed it.

'Right, let me just check that the coast is clear,' said Boadicea.

Jack could hear the workmen now. It sounded like they were making a thorough sweep of the whole scrapyard.

'Here, pretty pony!' one of them was shouting.

It was the man who'd told him to clear off.

'Come on – we've got a lovely sugar lump for you!' shouted the other workman.

'And then it's straight off to the knacker's yard. We'll take the meat for pet food and sell your bones down at the glue factory!' laughed the first one.

'Shh, Tony! Don't tell it that or it won't want to come to us,' said the second man.

'It's a HORSE! It can't understand what we're saying!'

Boadicea turned to Jack. 'Little do they know . . .' she said, with a wink.

The men were carrying big sticks and, as they prowled up and down the lines of old fridges and wrecked cars, they were

hitting them, trying to frighten Boadicea out.

'Quick,' said Boadicea. 'First stop, the outside toilet.'

'We haven't got time to go to the loo,' said Jack. 'They're coming this way.'

'I mean hide behind it, you buffoon,' she said.

'Oh . . .'

'Come on!' said Boadicea.

They quickly trotted over to the outside toilet, which was like a little shed, and hid behind it. They were just in the nick of time, for, as they darted behind, the workmen came round the corner into the stable.

'Cor, it stinks in here, doesn't it, Tony?'

'Too right, Jeff. Look, is that a fresh one?'

'How can you tell?'

'I dunno. Stick your finger in it – see if it's still warm. Haven't you watched any cowboy films?'

'Urgh, disgusting, I'm not doing that!'

The men went quiet for a moment and Jack wondered what they were doing. Then Tony giggled.

'Yeah, that's fresh,' said the one called Jeff. 'Oh blimey, me finger! Oh, it pongs!'

Tony burst out laughing.

'Never mind laughing – that pony is obviously around here somewhere. Get looking. There's good money in a horse carcass.'

Boadicea dared to peek round the corner and saw one of the men disappear behind Old Mr Mudge's office.

'He's gone the other way,' she said. 'Quick – towards that old ice-cream van.' And the pair of them dashed over to the wreck. From their side they could see through the windows and, although the windows were very dirty, they had a good view of the stables.

Jeff was using some straw to try and clean his smelly finger. When he'd finished, he seemed to look straight at the old ice-cream van; after a little thought, he began to stroll purposefully towards it.

'I tell you what,' said Jack. 'I'm really good at sneaking about and not being seen. Why don't I go down to the gate and open it, then I'll shout when I've done it and you can just dash down as fast as you can and escape on to the towpath?'

Boadicea regarded him with her imperious eye. 'You're not quite as stupid as you look, are you? Tally-ho!'

'I beg your pardon?' replied Jack.

'Tally-ho!' she said.

'What does that mean?'

Boadicea was getting quite exasperated. 'It means, "Off we go!" ' she said. 'Or "Get on with it" because he's nearly here!'

'OK, here I go,' said Jack.

As Jeff slowly approached the van, Jack slunk off. He was so small and so agile that he could flit about without being seen. He darted from shadow to shadow and, even if someone had been looking really hard, they would have thought they'd just seen the wind rustling in some dead leaves. In no time at all he reached the gate to the towpath.

'Here, Tony! I think I've found it. I think it's behind this old ice-cream van,' said Jeff.

'Dead right,' said Tony.

Boadicea turned sharply and was startled to find that Tony had crept up from nowhere and was standing right behind her.

'I think we've got it cornered. Have you got your rope ready?' said Jeff, approaching the van.

'I sure have,' said Tony. 'Look at that big fat

belly – we'll get hundreds of tins of dog food out of that.'

'THE GATE'S OPEN!'

shouted Jack at the top of his voice.

Just as the two men were closing in on Boadicea from both sides, with their ropes at the ready, she made a dash for it and forced her way between

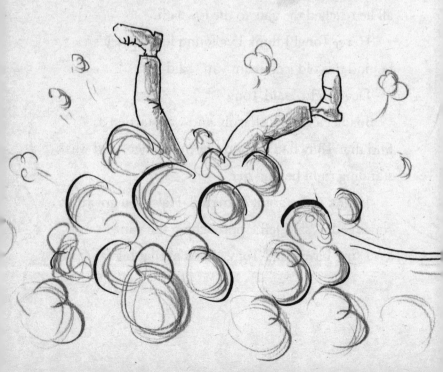

them. She was small but very determined, and the two men were knocked to the ground as she barged past. She ran as fast as she could – which was surprisingly speedy for a pony with such a round belly and such short legs – and sprinted through the open gate and along the towpath.

Jack could see the two men running after her, so he quickly darted through and locked the gate after him. He'd only just finished turning the key when they reached the gate.

'What are you doing, kid? Come on – give us the key!' they shouted, rattling the gate and trying to force it open.

'No, I won't,' said Jack.

Just then someone blew loudly on a whistle, and Jack looked up to see two police officers running down from the stables towards the gate.

'Oh blimey. We've been rumbled,' whispered Tony. He turned to one of the police officers and said, 'It's all right, guv! We were just collecting the pony to take him to the pony sanctuary, weren't we, Jeff?'

'That's right, we were,' said Jeff. 'Out of the goodness of our hearts.'

'It's not you we're after. It's the young lad,' said the officer, who came right up to the gate and smiled at Jack. 'Are you Jack Sampson?'

Jack was frozen to the spot; he didn't know what to say.

'You're not in any trouble, lad – it's just your auntie is really worried about you. She thought you might be here and she'd like us to take you home.'

'No!' shouted Jack. 'I'm not going back – I hate it there! They keep me in a cupboard and they want to send me to an orphanage!'

'I'm sure it's just a misunderstanding,' said the officer. 'Why don't you unlock the gate and we can have a little chat about it?'

'No, I won't!' said Jack, and he threw the key into the canal and ran down the towpath in the same direction as Boadicea, though she was already a long way ahead of him, galloping as fast as she could.

'Jack, stop!'

shouted the police
officer. But it was no
good. Jack had gone.
The other officer tried
to climb on to the first one's
shoulders to get over the
high wall, but the top was
protected with coils of
barbed wire and they
couldn't get past.

When Jack glanced
back, he saw that the
police officers had
got tangled up in the
barbed wire and that

Tony and Jeff were laughing at them.

Searching in the direction Boadicea had gone,
Jack could see a white speck in the distance, with
dust billowing up from her hooves as she raced
along. Jack thought two things: *She's much faster
at running than I imagined*, and *Surely she's got to stop
soon*. But Boadicea kept on galloping, and shortly
afterwards she disappeared out of sight round a
bend in the towpath.

CHAPTER

11

Jack kept running for ages and ages, trying to catch up with Boadicea. He ran for miles as the sun rose but saw no sign of her.

As he hurried along, the buildings began to thin out. Once or twice he thought he heard a police siren in the distance, but he hid behind walls and bushes until the noise went away, then came out and started running again.

The canal and its towpath led away from the city centre, through an industrial estate, a shopping mall and some housing estates. Finally it reached the countryside, with fields on both sides.

The sun beat down and seemed to sap all Jack's energy. He was getting very tired, but his only thoughts were to catch up with Boadicea and not get caught by the police.

Eventually Jack got a stitch and couldn't run any more. He was at a bend in the canal. The whole valley had suddenly opened up before him and he could see for miles ahead, but there was still no sign of Boadicea.

She must have run far, far away, he thought.

He sat down on the bank of the canal, feeling ever so slightly sorry for himself, and wondered what to do.

'Yoo-hoo, Jack,' came a loud whisper.

Jack turned. The whisper seemed to be coming from a large clump of trees behind him.

'Yes, that's right, you idiot – I'm in the trees. Good grief, what do you use for a brain?'

'Boadicea?' asked Jack.

'No, it's the Queen of Sheba,' said Boadicea

sarcastically. 'Of course it's me, you silly chuckaboo! Get in here, quickly, before they see you.'

'Before who sees me?' asked Jack as he walked into the clump of trees where Boadicea was hiding.

'The men from the glue factory!' said Boadicea, shuddering at the thought.

'But they got stuck in the junkyard, with the police officers,' said Jack. 'I locked the gate and threw the key in the canal.'

Boadicea looked at Jack, open-mouthed.

'You mean,' she said, 'you mean that I have run for miles . . . and miles . . . and miles . . . and *miles* . . . wearing my little hooves down to the bone . . . for absolutely no reason at all?'

'Well, you ran away so fast that I couldn't catch you,' said Jack.

'And what do you mean, police officers? I didn't see any. What were they doing there?'

'They were looking for me.'

'Why? What have you done?' asked Boadicea, suddenly alarmed.

'I think I've run away from home, though I'm not sure I really meant to. But, now that I have, I'm actually quite glad,' said Jack.

And he went on to explain about living with his aunt and uncle and his horrible cousin, and sleeping in a cupboard, and the incident with the smelly chicken nuggets, and locking himself in the bathroom, and his uncle threatening to send him to an orphanage.

'My stars and garters!' exclaimed Boadicea. 'What a beastly situation! I'm going to have to have a lie-down and a little cogitation about all this.'

Jack wasn't sure what a 'little cogitation' was, but he could see that she was very tired and he felt exhausted himself.

They settled down together in the clearing in the middle of the clump of trees and let the dappled sunshine warm their exhausted bodies. Jack rested his head on Boadicea's big belly, listening to her heartbeat, and they both lay there for a while, getting their breath back.

Boadicea was thinking about Jack's situation, and Jack was thinking about the fact that Boadicea could actually talk.

After a while Boadicea said, 'The truth is, I don't think very well when I'm peckish. I don't suppose you've got a spot of tiffin in your pocket, have you?'

'What's *a spot of tiffin*?' asked Jack.

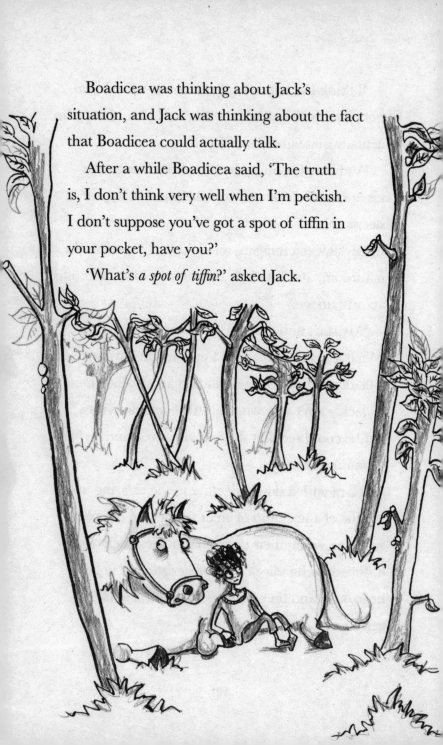

'Tiffin – you know, food – a handful of pony nuts perhaps?'

'No, sorry,' he replied.

'I've missed breakfast – one of the seven most important meals of the day,' she said. 'What are we going to eat?'

'Well, there's a field there, full of grass,' said Jack.

'Yes,' she said rather sniffily. 'Strictly *entre nous*, I think grass is rather overrated.'

'What does *entre nous* mean?' he asked.

'Heavens to Betsy, don't they teach you anything in school these days? It's French and means "between ourselves".'

Jack thought for a moment. 'What does *Heavens to Betsy* mean?' he asked.

Boadicea lifted her head and looked down her long nose, straight into Jack's face.

'Listen,' she said, 'if you're going to ask me to explain absolutely everything I say, you and I had better part company right now. *Comprendi?*'

Jack didn't say anything. He just nodded in agreement.

They both settled down to rest once more. But something was troubling Jack. There was so much he wanted to ask, but he didn't want to annoy Boadicea. He waited for as long as he could, so that it didn't seem like he was pestering her, and then he said, 'You know yesterday? When I came to the gates and shouted for you?'

'Yes,' said Boadicea, with a small sigh, keeping her eyes closed.

She didn't sound too annoyed, so Jack carried on.

'Why didn't you answer me?'

'Because the workmen were there, you numbskull. I'd just spent half an hour hiding from those fiendish ne'er-do-wells. I was hardly going to give myself away at the last minute, was I?'

'Oh, I see,' said Jack.

'And anyway,' said Boadicea, 'I knew I could get you to come to your bathroom window and see me whenever I wanted to. I've always had that power.'

'What?' asked Jack.

'Oh yes. I just stare at your window in the block of flats, and within a minute or two you always come and look.'

'No, that's what I do to you!' said Jack. 'I stare at the stable and you come out.'

'No, I stare, you come.'

'No, I do.'

'No, it's me.'

'It's me.'

'It's me.'

'It's me.'

'Smee,' she said as they got faster and faster.

'Smee.'

'Smee.'

'Smee.'

'Smee.'

'Smee.'

'Smee.'

'Me.'

'Me.'

'Me.'

'Me.'

'Me.'

'Me.'

Eventually they both broke into howls of laughter and then lay there, panting, with huge smiles on their faces.

'Well, perhaps it works both ways,' said Boadicea rather graciously.

'I've just had a brainwave,' said Jack. 'Maybe there's a farm near here where someone keeps a pony. If we asked nicely, they might give us some nuts.'

Boadicea fell silent.

Jack turned to look at her. She had an incredulous look on her face – her jaw was hanging open in an expression of total bafflement.

'What? What is it?' asked Jack, worried that something had gone very wrong.

When at last she could summon up the words, Boadicea spoke very slowly and deliberately.

'You think that *people* keep *horses*?'

Now it was Jack's turn to look confused.

'You don't think it's the other way round?' Boadicea continued.

'But . . .'

'Do I ever groom you?' interrupted Boadicea. 'Do I ever feed you? Do I ever go around picking up your poo?'

'Well, no,' said Jack.

'So who is keeping whom?' asked Boadicea.

'But humans ride horses, don't they?'

'Lawks-a-lordy, of course they do, but only if we want them to! Have you never seen us bucking someone off? If we don't want you to ride, you don't ride, old fruit – I think you'll find the decision is all ours.'

These ideas were new to Jack, but the more he thought about it, the more they seemed to make sense. Although it was still a bit puzzling.

'But don't people buy and sell horses?' he asked.

'Oh, occasionally we move about, looking for better service, better food, better stables. We like to travel and see the world, you know – we're not philistines. But we always get some human to take us there in a private horsebox – can you imagine how far we'd have to walk otherwise? And we don't do public transport.'

'I've never thought about it like that before,' said Jack.

'One wonders whether you do much thinking at all,' said Boadicea. 'Now, what are we going to do about food? We've definitely missed breakfast. It's probably at least elevenses time by now – the second most important meal of the day.'

Just at that moment a rabbit popped out of its burrow in the clump of trees. The rabbit saw Jack and Boadicea and stopped in its tracks.

'Ah, splendid, a local! He should know the lie of the land around here,' said Boadicea. Turning to the rabbit, she said, 'Good afternoon, Mr Rabbit, I'm afeared that we have strayed far from home and are a little unsure of our whereabouts. Could you perhaps direct us to some kind of hostelry where we might partake of board and lodging? I'm especially interested in the "board" part – pony nuts to be precise.'

The rabbit stared at Boadicea.

'What ails thee, Mr Rabbit? Hast thou lost thy voice?' asked Boadicea.

The rabbit lifted a paw and pointed at Jack as if to say, *What about him?*

'Great Scott! Forgive me, Mr Rabbit – I should have said! This young blot knows all about animals talking. There was a "situation" and I'm afraid I had to let the secret out. Good job I did though, because this young blighter saved my life – if it wasn't for him, I'd be at the glue factory by now. He's perfectly harmless.'

'Well, why didn't you say?' said the rabbit, eyeing Jack with less suspicion.

Jack slapped his hand to his forehead in astonishment. 'A talking rabbit!' he exclaimed, almost fainting with surprise.

'Why does it always

affect them like this?' asked the rabbit.

'I've no idea,' replied Boadicea. 'They seem to think that the world is theirs and that they know everything about it.'

'Yes, such a blinkered view,' said the rabbit. 'Now, you were asking about board and lodging?'

'Yes, absolutely, old bean. I'm most keen on locating a source of pony nuts. Having persuaded these poor sad humans to make them for us, it seems a shame not to eat as many as possible.'

'A talking rabbit!' said Jack again.

'Ignore him,' said Boadicea. 'He'll get over it in time.'

'Well,' said the rabbit, 'vis-à-vis the pony-nut predicament, I think you're in luck. The canal goes into a tunnel a little further along, but you'll come to a signpost which will direct you to a village called Penny Bridges. There you'll find some racing stables. To be honest, they don't have the best reputation, but I'm sure the horses will have ordered their humans to get a few pony nuts in.'

'Splendid fellow, many thanks,' said Boadicea. 'Come, Jack, we must press on – luncheon awaits!'

Boadicea strode out of the clump of trees on to the towpath. Jack straggled along behind, looking dazed and confused.

'A talking rabbit,' he said, glancing back, but the rabbit had already disappeared.

'Yes, so you've said. Several times. Try not to lose your onion, old chap. If you're going to be startled by this kind of thing, you may actually die of surprise before long. Now, I can see you're a bit unsteady on your feet, so why not hop on? That way we might get to a bit of nosebag sooner rather than later.'

Absent-mindedly Jack climbed on to Boadicea's back and she trotted off along the towpath.

'A talking rabbit,' said Jack again.

'Great Caesar's ghost,' muttered Boadicea.

CHAPTER

They walked along the towpath in
the direction the rabbit had
pointed, and after a
mile or so the canal
disappeared into a tunnel as
the rabbit had said. Running across
the top of the tunnel there was a road
and a signpost, as promised.

The signpost had three fingers.
One pointed to the right and
said COURTLY MANOR HOTEL, one
pointed to the left and said PRISON,
and the third pointed down a bridle
path and said PENNY BRIDGES.

'Ah, Penny Bridges is straight on along one of my private roads – splendid,' said Boadicea, trotting off down the bridle path.

Jack was glad that Boadicea had read the signs because he couldn't make them out at all. And he was still thinking about the fact that Boadicea could talk and about the rabbit . . . but his thoughts were interrupted by a huge clap of thunder.

Jack looked up, thinking it must be about to pour with rain, but there wasn't a cloud in the sky.

'Did you hear that thunder?' he asked.

'I'm afraid that wasn't thunder, old bean – that was my stomach rumbling,' said Boadicea. 'It's crying out for sustenance!'

'Well, there's lots of grass in these fields,' said Jack, pointing to either side of the bridle path.

'As I have previously indicated, I'm not overly fond of the green stuff.'

'Well, all these cows and sheep seem to like it,' said Jack.

'Yes, well, they're cows and sheep – they're

not exactly known for their refined tastes!' said
Boadicea.

Some of the sheep heard Boadicea as she
trotted past and looked at her with an expression
of alarm. It was a look which meant, *That pony has
just broken the rule about not speaking in front of humans.*

An old bull was idly leaning against a fence post,
chewing the cud, and, as they passed, Boadicea
said a very cheery 'Morning!'

The bull replied, 'Morning,' without paying
much attention to who he was talking to. When he
saw that Boadicea actually had a human on her
back, he looked perplexed.

'Oh no . . . sorry . . . er . . .' he said,
ashamed that he'd broken the rule,
and nervously looking
around to see if the
cows had heard him.

'A talking bull,' said Jack, quite gobsmacked.

'Oh, not again,' said Boadicea.

'But it talked!'

'Yes.'

Jack looked back at the bull, but he had already run off to hide his embarrassment.

Boadicea trotted on.

Jack thought to himself for a while and then asked, 'Can all animals talk?'

'Well, of course they can,' said Boadicea. 'We're not idiots, you know.'

Jack thought about this for a little while longer and then asked: 'And do you all speak English?'

'Well, most of us do. Obviously there are quite a number of migrating birds that fly in from Africa and other far-flung places, speaking Swahili or Russian or Arctic or some such foreign tongue, but generally we all speak English. I believe in most zoos they speak a kind of hotch-potch of all the languages mixed together, called Esperanto. Welsh mountain ponies like to stay bilingual, speaking a bit of Welsh here and there, and Highland cattle try to keep going with a bit of Gaelic, but in Britain we mostly speak English.'

'What about dogs and cats and mice?'

'Oh yes, all of them.'

Jack remembered the mice in his cupboard and realized they could understand everything he said. It made him feel warm inside.

'What about insects?' he asked.

'Well, that's an interesting case – apparently they can, but they have such small voices that I, for one, find them very difficult to hear.'

Jack and Boadicea reached the end of the bridle path and found themselves on the outskirts of Penny Bridges. They saw an old farm with a range of outbuildings. On the gate was a tatty old sign, with its paint peeling off.

'*Joe Sampson Racing Stables*,' said Boadicea, reading it out loud.

'I beg your pardon?' said Jack in alarm.

'*Joe Sampson Racing Stables*,' repeated Boadicea.

'Joe Sampson? Are you sure that's what it says?' asked Jack.

'Of course, old fruit – read it for yourself.'

'But J-Joe Sampson . . .' stammered Jack. 'Joe Sampson's my dad!'

'Your father owns the stables? Well, that's splendid news!' said Boadicea. 'Why didn't you mention this before? This is top-hole! He'll give us a proper feed and no mistake. Ooh, I wonder if

he has any sugar lumps —'

'No, no, no, you don't understand,' Jack replied. 'He *is* my dad, but he left my mum before I was born. I've never even met him.'

And Jack went on to explain the whole situation. He told Boadicea about his mother and Aunt Violet growing up at Broadacre Farm; about his dad gambling it away; and about his mother being put in prison for stealing from the hotel.

'So that's why you have to live with your beastly relatives?' said Boadicea.

'That's right,' said Jack, and he told Boadicea all about his mum being innocent; and how the disk from the security cameras would prove it if only someone could find it; and about the secret room; and that he wished he could do something to help his mum.

'Well, heavens to Betsy, this is a rum situation, my little chuckaboo.'

But Boadicea's train of thought was interrupted by another clap of thunder that came from her hungry belly.

'Oh dear, I'm almost too faint from hunger to think at all,' she continued. 'If I don't get some tuck pretty sharpish, I may waste away entirely.'

Jack looked at Boadicea. Although her tummy was rumbling with the sound of a jumbo jet taking off, she was the same size she'd always been. Her belly still hung low, almost brushing the ground, and the idea that she might be wasting away seemed ridiculous to Jack.

'I think we'd better investigate the stables,' said Boadicea, turning towards them.

'I think it'd be best if I went in on my own first,' said Jack. 'I'm small and quick and I can have a look about without being seen.'

Boadicea gave Jack a quizzical look. 'And you think *I* will be seen?'

'Well, it's more likely.'

Boadicea looked slightly miffed. 'Are you suggesting that I'm fat?'

'Er . . .' mumbled Jack.

'Because I am *not* fat,' said Boadicea indignantly. 'Indeed I am *not*. Have you seen the breed book on ponies? This is how Shetlands are supposed to be. We are hardy and strong, with short, muscular necks; a compact, stocky body; and short, strong legs. And you will find that a short, broad back and deep girth are universal characteristics. As is a springy stride.'

As she said this, she strode up and down with an exaggerated spring in her step to show what she meant.

'Yes, and you look very lovely,' said Jack. 'But you've got to admit that I'm very skinny and small, and that I'm good at hiding and flitting about from one place to another. Remember how I ran down from the stable to unlock the gate at Old Mr Mudge's place? Those men never saw me.'

As Boadicea was weighing this up, a battered old pickup truck came through the village. It was heading towards them.

'Quick, hide!' said Jack, and they both leapt into a ditch.

Peeking out of the ditch, Jack could see the pickup truck getting closer. At first it looked like no one was driving it because he couldn't see anyone

behind the wheel. But as it got nearer he spotted two hands on the steering wheel, and as it turned into the stables he could make out a very small man. He was so small he could barely see over the dashboard, and he looked very cross.

'You stay here!' said Jack to Boadicea, and without waiting for a reply he followed in the cloud of dust that the pickup truck left in its wake.

CHAPTER

The cloud of dust thrown up by the pickup truck allowed Jack to sneak into the yard unseen. He found a hiding place behind a couple of hay bales and looked out.

He'd seen racing yards on TV – they were bright and bustling places, filled with well-groomed horses and happy, smiling people. They were always spick and span, and everything was kept in perfect order.

This yard was the exact opposite. It was grim and grimy and there were only three sad-looking horses. The handful of people tending to them looked totally miserable too. Stable doors were hanging off their hinges; many of the windows were broken; and two ravens clattered around on the rooftops, looking as if they were waiting for something to die.

Jack saw the man from the pickup truck rush into a rundown Portakabin in the corner of the yard, and seconds later he heard the sound of the racing channel blaring out of a TV.

'Come on, Firecracker!' the little man shouted.

'Come on! Come on! Run faster!

Why are you third? I've got a hundred quid on you to win! You stupid, stupid horse!'

Jack ghosted round the edge of the yard and hid behind an old water barrel next to the Portakabin window. He carefully stood on tiptoe and peeked through. The little man was bobbing up and down, pretending to ride a horse, just like Jack did when he watched the racing. But he didn't look like he

was having any fun – his eyes were dark and scared, and his face was set into an angry snarl.

'*And first past the post it's Trick of the Light,*' said the commentator. '*Closely followed by Moonshadow and Roaring Boy, and slipping back to fourth place is the favourite, Firecracker . . .*'

The little man went berserk. His face turned purple with rage and he ran out into the yard, kicking everything he could find. He kicked a bucket of water, he kicked his pickup truck, and he kicked a wheelbarrow full of horse poo that an unhappy-looking girl was wheeling round to the muck heap. The wheelbarrow tipped over and all the horse poo fell out.

'What'd you do that for?' shouted the little man at the unhappy-looking girl.

'Steady on, Joe,' said an old man with a limp, who was leading a horse with a limp out of one of the stables.

Joe! thought Jack. *The little man is Joe! That's my dad!*

'Why don't you look where you're going, you idiot?' Joe shouted at the girl, who was now starting to cry.

'It wasn't her fault, Joe,' said the old man.

'You stay out of it, Dad!' yelled Joe. 'And what's wrong with that horse?'

'He's got a bit of laminitis,' said the old man.

'Well, get rid of it, sell it, shoot it, whatever – it's costing me food and vet's fees and I don't need crocked horses. I only want winners. Where's Morning Glory?'

A nervous-looking apprentice jockey emerged from the best stable. He was leading a rather fine-looking horse.

'She's here, Mr Sampson,' he said. 'I saddled her up because you said you were going to take her for a gallop this morning. But you spent so long at the betting shop I thought you'd changed your mind.'

'This is the horse,' said Joe, calming down a bit as he stroked Morning Glory's forehead and rubbed her muzzle. 'We might as well sell the rest of them for cat food – this is the only one that's any good. This is the one that's going to win the Grand National, aren't you, girl? And once I win the Grand National I'll be rich, and I'll be able to live the good life again, instead of slumming it here in these rotten old stables.'

'They may be rotten old stables, but the question is – has he got any pony nuts for the starving friend of his long-lost son?' whispered Boadicea, who had crept up behind Jack.

Jack turned round, startled, knocking the water barrel over as he did so.

'Boadicea!' he whispered back. 'What are you doing here?'

'Well, I was getting bored. And frightfully hungry. Uh-oh . . .' said Boadicea, pointing her head at the barrel as it rolled down the slight slope into the yard.

The barrel was picking up speed and heading straight towards Joe, who had his back to it. Everyone else in the yard could see it hurtling towards him, but no one dared to say a word because they didn't want to make him cross by talking.

The barrel crashed into the back of Joe's legs and sent him flying

up into the air. He landed in a crumpled heap, but quickly got up to shout at whoever was to blame.

'Was that you?' he yelled when he saw Jack and Boadicea by the side of the Portakabin. 'What are you doing here, kid? This is private property. You're not allowed in here.

Get off
my land!'

Boadicea nudged Jack out into the yard and whispered so that none of the other humans could hear, 'Tell him.'

'Please, sir,' said Jack, shaking with fear. 'I think you're my dad.'

'What?'

'I think you're my dad.'

'What you talking about? I ain't got no kids. I

don't want no kids. Never wanted no kids. So I ain't got no kids. Clear off before I call the police.'

'What's your name, boy?' asked the old man.

'My name's Jack. Jack Sampson.'

'Oh, how convenient!' said Joe. 'Your surname's Sampson, so suddenly you think we're related and you can just swan in here and ask for money – is that it? Well, you ain't getting any!'

'Don't be so hard on him, Joe,' said the old man. 'He's only a kid.'

'I don't want any money,' said Jack meekly.

'Whaddya want then?' snarled Joe.

Jack faltered, but Boadicea gave him a nudge from behind.

'It's just that I'm in a bit of trouble because my mum's not around and –'

'Who's your mum?' interrupted the old man.

'Her name is Bridget,' said Jack. 'Bridget Sampson. She used to live at Broadacre Farm.'

The old man's eyes opened wide in recognition.

'Oh, I ain't got time for this kind of nonsense!'

shouted Joe. 'It's a pack of lies. I ain't got no kid. And I don't want no kid. Now get lost, cos the next race is about to start and I've got a hundred quid on the forty-to-one outsider. If it comes in first, I'll win four thousand quid!'

Joe rushed into the Portakabin to watch the race. The telly was turned up to full volume and everyone could hear the commentator saying, '*They're under starter's orders . . . and they're off!*'

As the rest of the yard went back to work, the old man limped up to Jack and bent down to get a closer look at him.

'So you're Bridget's boy, are you? I heard tell she had a little one after she and Joe parted ways, but I never knew for sure. But you're the spitting image of your dad, that's for sure. There's no mistaking it. And do you know what else?' he asked.

'You're my grandad,' said Jack.

'Well, bless my soul, how did you work that out?'

'I heard him call you dad,' said Jack.

'Did you now? Well, what about that? Here,

come and give your old grandad a hug,' said
Grandad, folding Jack into his arms. 'All this time
I've had a grandson and never knew. Oh, this is a
happy day.'

Jack hugged his grandad back. He smelled
of pipe tobacco and freshly mown hay. They
held each other for a while, listening to the race
as it blared out of the television speakers in the
Portakabin, then his grandad looked up and said,
'Is that your pony?'

'Well, she's not *my* pony,' said Jack. 'She doesn't *belong* to me. But we're very good friends.'

'Good friends, hey? That's a lovely way to be with an animal. If only your dad could learn that. What's the pony's name?'

'Boadicea,' said Jack.

'Boadicea,' said Grandad. 'What a fine name. I bet she's hungry, isn't she?'

Boadicea looked up with an expectant smile on her face.

'How did you know that?' asked Jack.

'Shetlands are always hungry,' said Grandad. 'That's why they're so fat.'

Boadicea's smile turned sharply into a look of haughty indignation.

'But if you look in the breed book,' said Jack, 'I think you'll find that a short, broad back and deep girth are universal catacaristics. As is a springy stride.'

Boadicea beamed at Jack with pride.

'That's true enough,' said Grandad. 'Well said. Now come on, let's get her some pony nuts.'

He shuffled over to the store where the feed bins were kept, with Jack and Boadicea following. Boadicea trotted along with a pronounced springy stride and a very big smile on her face.

Jack's grandad gave Boadicea three scoops of pony nuts.

'I know Shetlands,' he laughed. 'Two scoops are never enough.'

Jack and his grandad looked on as Boadicea gratefully dropped her head into the feed bucket and chomped away. They could hear the sound of the race coming from the Portakabin. And they could hear Joe getting more and more furious. It was obvious that the horse he had put a bet on wasn't doing very well.

'Come on, Fortune Cookie! What's the matter with you?' he bellowed at the TV. 'Just whip it!

Whip it and whip it and whip it and whip it! It's the only language they understand!'

'*We're into the final furlong now,*' said the commentator, '*and it's Trip of the Tongue, followed by Star Gazer and, behind Star Gazer, Lily the Pink is making a run on the outside. The rest of the field are tightly bunched in the chasing pack, and losing ground at the back, looking very sorry for himself, is Fortune Cookie . . .*'

Jack and his grandad could hear Joe throwing things about in anger as Fortune Cookie failed to make up any ground, and when the race came to an end Joe started screaming and crying like a two-year-old having a tantrum. But then the sound of the race programme came to an abrupt stop and a new voice blared out of the speakers.

'*We interrupt this programme to make an urgent appeal for the whereabouts of a missing boy. He is small and wiry, and accompanied by a white Shetland pony. Police are offering a reward to anyone who finds him. While the description of the boy is somewhat hazy, the pony is said to be instantly recognizable because it is so incredibly fat –*'

The sound of the TV suddenly stopped altogether and Joe rushed out of the Portakabin, scanned the yard, saw Jack near the feed store and ran over.

'So you're a snivelling little runaway, are you? Well, you're coming with me,' he said, grabbing Jack by the arm and pulling him over to the pickup truck. 'Oh yeah, a reward! Well, maybe I *will* make some money today.'

'Now, Joe, don't be too hasty,' said Grandad. 'He's Bridget's boy. Your son. Can't you see the resemblance?'

'Why do I have to keep saying it? I ain't got no kids!' shouted Joe, bundling Jack into the truck and slamming the door. 'Now leave me in peace while I drive to the police station and pick up the reward.'

He stomped round to the driver's side of the truck, but, just as he opened the door and was about to climb in, a large bundle of white shouting,

'Bombs away!'

barrelled into him, knocking him to the ground. It was Boadicea, of course. She whinnied and neighed as she ran round to the passenger side, and suddenly the other horses in the yard broke away from their handlers and rushed towards Joe where he lay on the ground.

Jack opened the passenger door.

'On my back!' whispered Boadicea.

Joe was rising to his feet again and made to run round and stop Jack escaping, but the other horses crowded round him.

'**Out of it!** Get out of it, you **stupid** nags!'

railed Joe.

But by this time Boadicea, with Jack on board, was already dashing out of the yard. As they sped past Grandad, he said, 'Good on you, lad. Head for the Dark Wood – they'll never find you there.'

Boadicea and Jack hightailed it out of the yard and into the fields. In the distance they could see a dark, forbidding wood and they galloped towards it, with the sound of Joe's shouts gradually receding in their ears.

CHAPTER

14

The closer they got to the wood, the scarier it became. It was an ancient woodland, full of gnarled old trees. It stood high up on the side of the valley, and the wind had blown all the trees in one direction, so that even when it wasn't blowing the trees were still bent over.

The ground beneath them was rocky and uneven, and the boulders and tree trunks were covered in a thick carpet of moss because the tree canopy was so dense that hardly any light came in.

Boadicea picked her way carefully through the underbrush and rocks, but the further they got into the wood, the harder it became, and after a while they had to admit that they were completely lost.

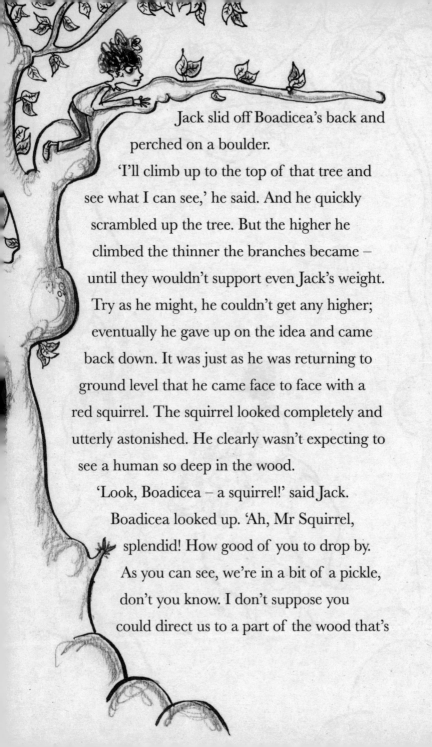

Jack slid off Boadicea's back and perched on a boulder.

'I'll climb up to the top of that tree and see what I can see,' he said. And he quickly scrambled up the tree. But the higher he climbed the thinner the branches became – until they wouldn't support even Jack's weight. Try as he might, he couldn't get any higher; eventually he gave up on the idea and came back down. It was just as he was returning to ground level that he came face to face with a red squirrel. The squirrel looked completely and utterly astonished. He clearly wasn't expecting to see a human so deep in the wood.

'Look, Boadicea – a squirrel!' said Jack.

Boadicea looked up. 'Ah, Mr Squirrel, splendid! How good of you to drop by. As you can see, we're in a bit of a pickle, don't you know. I don't suppose you could direct us to a part of the wood that's slightly less . . . well, slightly less woody?'

The squirrel looked at Boadicea and his little jaw dropped even further.

'Oh, the talking thing,' said Boadicea. 'I'm sorry, I keep forgetting. This little chap – Jack is his name – well, he sort of saved my life, you see. But in order to get him to do that I had to break the silly old code. Sorry and everything, but that's how it is. Anyway, the upshot is that he knows all about horses being able to speak.'

The squirrel looked at Jack, then back at Boadicea. 'That's all very well,' he said rather crossly, 'but he doesn't know about squirrels talking, does –'

The squirrel stopped mid-sentence and clapped his tiny front paw to his forehead.

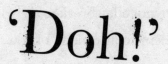'Doh!'

Jack laughed. 'It's all right, Mr Squirrel, I promise I won't tell anyone. I don't have any friends anyway, so it's not very likely.'

'He really is very unpopular,' said Boadicea, trying to be helpful. 'He has no friends at school. He lives with his smelly uncle, his drippy aunt and a horrible cousin who bullies him. Even his dad hates him.'

The expression on the squirrel's face suddenly changed to one of pity and sympathy. 'Your own father hates you?' he asked.

'Well, he doesn't seem to like me very much,' Jack replied. 'Though to be fair he didn't know that I existed until about half an hour ago. So I think he was a bit surprised.'

'However, he was prepared to dob you in to the police,' said Boadicea.

'The police? You're not a lawbreaker, are you?' said the squirrel, suddenly concerned. 'I know everyone thinks the wood is a lawless place after that terrible book *The Wind in the Willows* gave us such a bad reputation, but we're actually very law-abiding.'

'I'm not a lawbreaker – it's just that I've run away from home. Except that I haven't because I haven't really got a home. And I had to rescue Boadicea anyway . . .'

Jack and Boadicea went on to explain the whole situation to the squirrel: about Jack's mum being in prison, about the necklace robbery at the hotel and not being able to get hold of the security disk, about Old Mr Mudge and Lightning, about the two men and the knacker's yard, about Broadacre, and about the shenanigans at Joe Sampson's stables.

And Boadicea added a little bit about not getting enough to eat and being on the very edge of actual starvation, and how, if the squirrel could point them in the direction of some pony nuts, she would be eternally grateful.

'Well, well, well!' said the squirrel. 'You two certainly have had an interesting time of late . . .'

Just at that moment the three of them heard a twig snap and, turning to look, they saw Jack's grandad fall into their little patch of wood.

'Grandad!'

shouted Jack, dashing to help him get up off the ground.

The squirrel darted a look at Boadicea, as if to say, *Do you think he heard us talking?*

'Are you all right, Grandad? Have you hurt yourself?' asked Jack.

Grandad got up and dusted the moss off his knees.

'Oh, I'm fine. I'm absolutely fine. Couldn't be finer,' he said, a beaming smile on his face, as he looked round at Boadicea and the squirrel. 'Well, I never. Never in all my days. I never thought I'd hear it with my own ears. I've heard the stories, of course. There's always been rumours and such like.

I've always had my suspicions. But I never thought I'd actually hear it for real. *From the horse's mouth*, so to speak. But now I have, now I've heard it, good and proper – a pony and a squirrel . . . talking!'

The squirrel buried his head in his paws. Boadicea looked glumly on with an *Oh dear* expression on her face.

'Oh, Grandad, you weren't supposed to hear that,' said Jack.

'Ah, I could see it was a bit of a private chinwag,' said Grandad. 'That's why I held back. But then that damp bit of wood gave way. And, well, here I am. Can't really un-hear it, can I? Not that I'd want to.'

'This is your grandfather?' the squirrel asked Jack.

'Yes,' Jack replied.

'Well, it's just too much. It's really a step too far. It's opened up a whole can of worms. I'm afraid I'm going to have to swear you both into the animal code,' continued the squirrel.

'Top-hole idea!' agreed Boadicea.

'Raise your right paw and repeat after me,' said the squirrel. 'Sorry, not paw. What is it you call them? Not *hoof*, not *foot*. It's –'

'Hand,' interrupted Jack.

'Hand! That's the one,' said the squirrel. 'Raise your right hand and repeat after me: *I solemnly swear to uphold the animal code.*'

'I solemnly swear to uphold the animal code,' repeated Jack and Grandad, raising their right hands.

'*To keep secret the secrets of the animal kingdom.*'

'To keep secret the secrets of the animal kingdom.'

'*And never divulge how smart we are to the stupid humans, who would only use this information against us.*'

'And never divulge how smart you are to the stupid humans, who would only use this information against you.'

'And I'm afraid this last bit is in squirrel, so simply repeat after me: eeahu scree ki kaka.'

'Eeahu scree ki kaka,' said Jack and his grandad, as carefully as possible.

'Sker pwick ti cho.'

'Sker pwick ti cho,' they echoed.

'Excellent – now, should you ever break this promise, the entire animal kingdom will come down upon you. And I promise you that can be very nasty.'

'This really is uncommonly decent of you, Mr Squirrel, old bean,' said Boadicea.

'Yes, it is, isn't it?' replied the squirrel, rather tersely. 'And for your information my name is actually Mr Nutcase; Squirrel Nutcase. Now, if you'll all wait here, I will alert the rest of the woodland creatures and see if we can't help you out of your predicament.'

And with that the squirrel darted off into the woods, chirruping and chirping to alert the other squirrels as he went.

'Now, if you don't mind me saying so,' said Grandad to Jack, 'I did overhear you talking about your poor mother and her being accused of stealing that necklace from the Courtly Manor Hotel. I know that hotel. It's just on the other side of the woods here. I spent a year working there when Joe went bust once. That's always been a rum old place. No one who's worked there has ever been happy. That Mrs Scrimshank, who runs it, whenever she wants to get out of paying someone their holiday pay, she sacks them. And, if she can't think of a good enough excuse for sacking them, she'll say they've been thieving. She's a right old vinegar knickers and no mistake.'

Jack giggled.

'What are you laughing about?' said Grandad.

'You said vinegar knickers,' said Jack.

'By Jove, I haven't heard that in years,' said Boadicea. 'What a delightful expression.'

'Another expression!' said Jack. 'What does it mean?'

'Well, it means someone who's not very nice, someone who's never happy except when someone else is unhappy,' said Grandad. 'Now I've had a thought. I'm thinking that, with the help of Boadicea here and all her friends, we might be able to get into the hotel and maybe find the secret room . . .'

CHAPTER

15

Jack had the best afternoon and evening.

True to his word, Mr Nutcase brought the leaders of all the woodland animals together, to see how they could help Jack.

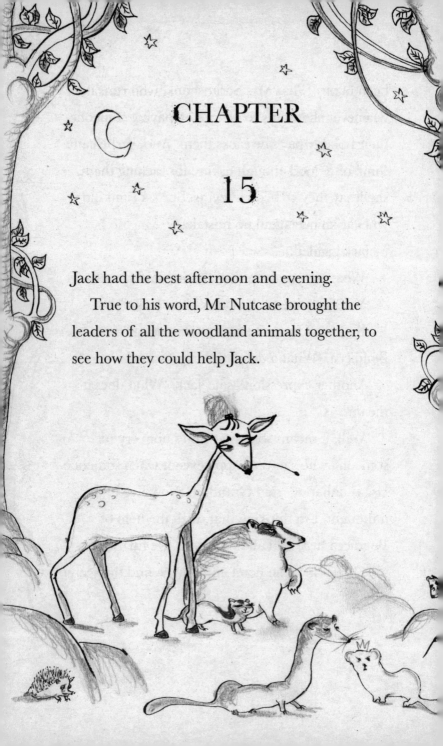

Jack met Stripy the badger; Gigi Golightly the deer; Archibald Stink the weasel; Freddie Fox; Dean the pine marten; Boris the wild boar; Fenella Ferret; Fat Matt the rat; and Lady Ermine the stoat.

He also met Allan Poe the crow; Maggie the magpie; and a bee called Sting. And last to arrive – in fact, he arrived halfway through the meeting – was a hedgehog called Mr Snufflepants.

Grandad was overjoyed to meet them all and to have the opportunity to actually *speak* to them.

He asked lots of questions he'd always wanted the answers to: he asked Maggie the magpie how long it took to build a nest – 'forty to fifty days'; he asked Stripy the badger what slugs actually tasted like – 'like the most succulent of savoury snacks, full of the flavours of mushrooms and truffles'; he asked Mr Snufflepants how he knew when it was time to hibernate – 'I just feel very, very, very tired'; and he asked the squirrels whether they always remembered where they'd buried their nuts.

'Oh, absolutely,' said Mr Nutcase. 'I'm aware that some idiot humans think we lose half the nuts we bury, but we don't; we remember them all. In fact, you're sitting on one of my many hidey-holes right this moment.'

Grandad looked at the ground beneath him and, after poking at it with a stick, found a pile of nuts!

'Nuts?' said Boadicea. 'Could you possibly spare

me a couple? I'm sort of on the famished side of
starving.'

But they were hazelnuts, not pony nuts, and
once she'd got them in her mouth she decided they
weren't really her cup of tea. She stood
there with a mouth full of half-
chewed nuts, not sure how
to get rid of them without
being rude.

'They probably just need
a bit of sweetening,' said a very, very
tiny voice. It was Sting the bee.

He gave her some honey to go with
them and, after a few tentative chews,
Boadicea decided she had never eaten anything
quite so delicious! She went on to eat all the nuts
in the hidey-hole and, although Mr Nutcase wasn't
totally unhappy about it, he wasn't particularly
happy either.

Eventually the meeting was called to order.
Mr Nutcase said that as Jack had been sworn in to

the animal code it was their duty to help him, and all the animals agreed. They decided that the best way to do this was to find the missing security disk so that Jack could get his mum out of prison.

Grandad told them all about the layout of the hotel, about the security cameras and Mrs Scrimshank's office, and a plan of action was drawn up for a raid on the hotel the next morning.

'Breakfast time is best,' said Mr Nutcase. 'They'll all be busy eating and we shall have surprise on our side.'

Boadicea was a little concerned at the timing of the raid.

'Do you mean actually *at* breakfast time?' she asked. 'Because that's all very well and what have you, and I'm all for the element of surprise, but, if we're going to be doing the raid at precisely breakfast time, when will *we* eat *our* breakfast? Do you see what I mean? I'm not sure I can face all the shenanigans on an empty stomach.'

Eventually it was agreed that Boadicea would

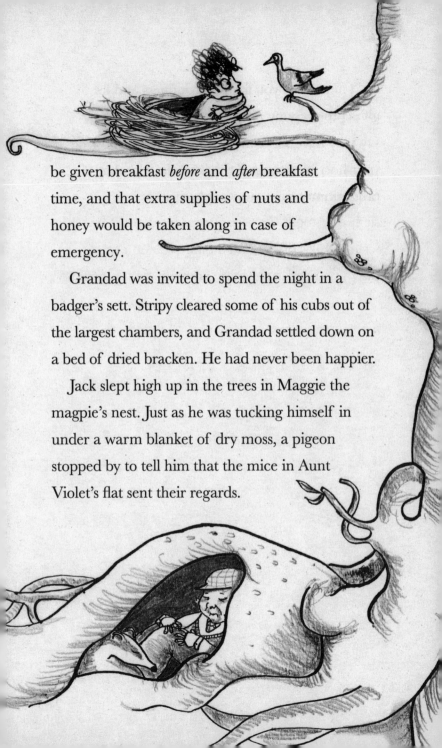

be given breakfast *before* and *after* breakfast
time, and that extra supplies of nuts and
honey would be taken along in case of
emergency.

Grandad was invited to spend the night in a
badger's sett. Stripy cleared some of his cubs out of
the largest chambers, and Grandad settled down on
a bed of dried bracken. He had never been happier.

Jack slept high up in the trees in Maggie the
magpie's nest. Just as he was tucking himself in
under a warm blanket of dry moss, a pigeon
stopped by to tell him that the mice in Aunt
Violet's flat sent their regards.

'They thank you for your kindness and for giving them pony nuts,' said the pigeon. 'They say they have some interesting evidence showing your horrible cousin Kelly is stealing football programmes from your cupboard!'

CHAPTER

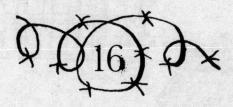

The next morning, at breakfast time, Jack, Grandad, Mr Nutcase and Boadicea (having already eaten, but still munching) emerged from the edge of the Dark Wood and stood in the cover of the trees. In front of them lay the perfectly manicured gardens of the Courtly Manor Hotel.

Not a leaf was out of place – everything was trimmed and tended and very tidy. There were neat box hedges dividing the flower beds, ornamental fountains, and enormous bushes cut into the shapes of lions and unicorns. It couldn't have looked any less like the Dark Wood.

In the middle of the gardens stood the hotel itself: an enormous stately home – all windows and

flagpoles and battlements, with a sweeping marble
staircase leading up to the front door.

At the bottom of the stairs, standing to
attention, were two porters dressed in purple
uniforms festooned with rows of brass buttons.

'Oh bother, peacocks!' said Mr Nutcase.

'No, I think they're just young chaps in uniform,' said Grandad.

'No, *real* peacocks,' said Mr Nutcase, jabbing his little paw in the direction of a pair of actual peacocks strutting up and down one of the paths.

'Can't you talk to them and get them to help us?' asked Grandad.

The squirrel screwed up his face in disdain.

'No,' he said. 'Peacocks are like police horses and Alsatians – dirty snitchers – they're always on the side of the humans. If we don't get to them first, they'll give the game away with their silly "piaowing".'

Mr Nutcase made a sharp *Come here* signal with his tail and another squirrel scurried out of the Dark Wood to stand at his side, ready for orders.

'Peacocks,' said Mr Nutcase, looking more and more like a small, furry army general. 'Ask the ferrets to scoot along that hedge and keep the peacocks quiet. Don't kill them – we're not savages – just threaten to pull out all their ridiculous feathers if they start squawking.'

The smaller squirrel saluted and ran back to deliver his orders.

In no time at all Jack saw Fenella and her ferrets dashing into the garden, keeping low, using the box hedges as cover.

They were soon out of sight, but Jack knew exactly where they were when there was a commotion in the garden and the peacocks suddenly disappeared from view. After a few seconds he could see Fenella poking her head above the hedge, waving a solitary peacock feather.

'Jolly good show!' said Boadicea.

'Surprise is our chief weapon,' said Mr Nutcase. 'We can't allow anything to warn of our approach. The next thing is to take out the exterior security cameras.'

Mr Nutcase made a loud

skiiieeew!

noise, and a horde of small animals suddenly stuck their heads up above the battlements on the roof of the hotel.

'Is that Dean and the pine martens?' asked Jack.

'Yes, indeed,' answered Mr Nutcase. 'They're the ones for this job. They're the most agile animals in the wood, even if they are a bit shy. Just watch.'

Jack looked on as the pine martens started to lower each other over the edge of the building. They hung on to each other's ankles and formed a long chain, and Dean, the one on the end, was able to bite through the cable coming out of the back of the security camera.

A second line of pine martens was disabling the security camera at the far end of the building.

'Excellent,' said Mr Nutcase. 'Now to distract the guards by the front door – this is a job for the deer.'

He waved his big bushy tail and made a loud noise in squirrel language:

'Skeeopp, skeeopp!'
'Peechoo, peechoo!' came a reply

from further along the edge of the wood, and
a young squirrel waved Gigi Golightly and her
small herd of deer out into the formal gardens.
They casually made their way towards
an immaculate bed of tulips . . . and
started eating them!

'The beautiful thing is that Gigi and
her friends actually think of tulips as
a kind of delicacy anyway,'
said Mr Nutcase. 'But keep
an eye on the guards.'

Jack turned to see the two porters in their shiny uniforms look on in alarm as the deer started munching away. They rushed from their posts at the bottom of the stairs and ran towards the deer, trying to shoo them off.

'When will the humans learn?' sighed Mr Nutcase. 'They're such dear little creatures but really quite dim.'

'Isn't it funny – the way they run!' laughed Boadicea, and all the animals chuckled along with her.

Mr Nutcase summoned the rest of his squirrel messengers from within the wood and gave them their orders.

'Right, chaps, the coast is clear, so here's the plan: I want Lady Ermine and the stoats in the upstairs bedrooms keeping the chambermaids busy, and Archibald and his weasels in the kitchen distracting the cooks. It's human "breakfast time", so all the guests will be in the dining room. Isn't it funny how they limit their eating to just three times a day?'

All the squirrels laughed in agreement. Boadicea would have laughed too, but her mouth was full of nuts and honey.

'The rats are waiting in the sewers and they'll work best in the dining room. I don't know why humans are so scared of them – it's we squirrels they really want to look out for!'

'Too right!' said one of the other squirrels, punching the air with his tiny paw.

'Squirrels rule!' agreed another, holding his front paws up like a boxer to show off his biceps. 'Check out these guns!'

'All these diversions will lay the hotel open to our main attack through the front door: I want the heavy mob – Stripy and his badgers and Boris with his wild boars – right in at reception,' Nutcase continued. 'We need to barge our way through to the office. Our elite force – the squirrels, of course – will tackle Mrs Scrimshank in the office, taking Grandad, Jack and Boadicea with them, to look for the secret room.'

'What about the foxes?' asked one of the other squirrels.

'They can do what they do best – empty the bins and throw the rubbish all over the place,' Mr Nutcase replied.

'And the hedgehogs?' asked another.

'Is Mr Snufflepants here yet?'

'They've just arrived.'

'They're so slow . . .' sighed Mr Nutcase. 'Get them to follow along behind and mop up any pockets of resistance. Which just leaves the magpies and the crows to dive-bomb any stragglers, with the swarm of bees in reserve for emergencies.

CHAPTER

17

Two minutes later, the hotel was in a state of complete uproar.

The pine martens crawled in through the upstairs windows and set to work ripping the sheets and blankets off the beds, tearing open the pillows and letting the feathers fly all over the place, while Lady Ermine and the stoats chased the chambermaids up and down the corridors.

The weasels sneaked in through the cellar windows and caused havoc in the kitchens, upsetting all the boiling saucepans, ripping open sacks of flour to create a snowstorm, and throwing the chefs' hats on to the cookers where they caught fire.

The diners in the dining room were
absolutely horrified when hundreds of rats
suddenly emerged from behind radiators
and through holes in the skirting boards. In
no time at all they were running up people's
legs, climbing on to the tables and knocking
over bowls of cereal and pots of tea.

The guests were screaming and didn't know
which way to run. A particularly confident
rat stood up on his hind legs on the table
and gave one of the ladies a big kiss on the
lips, and she fainted from fright.

The badgers and wild boars crashed through into the entrance hall, and within seconds the place looked like a bomb had gone off. Every piece of furniture lay broken and mangled, and the front desk was rammed by the boars until it was just a pile of matchsticks. The reception staff fled for their lives, running out of the hotel and along the drive as fast as they could.

The concierge, a brave man who had been in the army, stayed at his post a little longer and tried to call the police.

'Hello, this is the Courtly Manor Hotel. We're under attack . . .' he said, but suddenly the line went dead, and he looked up just in time to see Fenella the ferret biting through the telephone cable. Then he too fled as fast as his chubby little legs would take him.

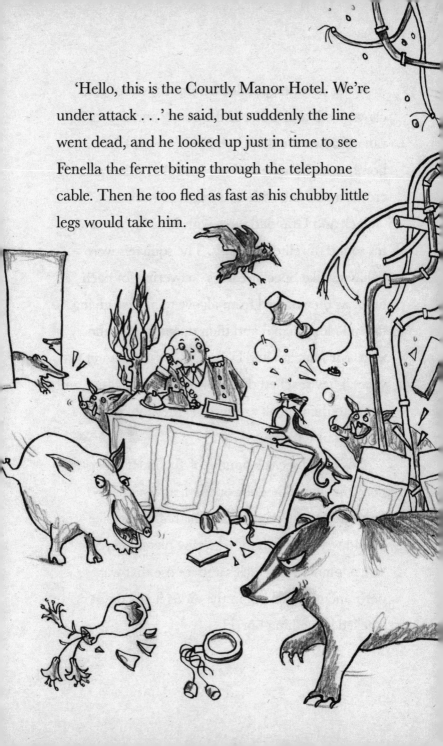

It was absolute pandemonium – a sea of fur, claws, teeth and tails. All the guests and the staff ran off down the drive, where they were dive-bombed by Maggie and her magpies, Allan and his crows, and Sting with his swarm of bees.

Jack and Grandad were with Mr Nutcase and his squad of 'elite' squirrels. The squirrels were behaving like Special Forces – covering for each other as they moved from alcove to alcove, giving the 'all-clear' signal and then moving on to the next. Mr Nutcase had even found a small beret to wear. They reached the door to the inner office and clung to the wall all around it – they looked like a furry picture frame.

Jack could see the handle of the inner office door turning. The door opened, and suddenly there was Mrs Scrimshank. She had a face like an old wrinkled lemon, with tiny piercing eyes, sharp, pointed spectacles and a nose that was permanently stuck up in the air as if she'd just smelled something horrid.

'What on earth is all this racket?'

she screeched. 'I shall sack all the people responsible with no holiday pay!'

In a flash the squirrels were upon her. They pinned her to the wall – two squirrels stretching themselves across each of her arms and legs and digging into the oak panelling with their claws, like living manacles.

As soon as she was secured, Mr Nutcase gave a signal, and Jack, Grandad and Boadicea ran through into the office.

'Right, lad, where's this secret room, do you think?' asked Grandad. He tapped on the walls to see if any of the wooden panels sounded hollow.

'I recognize you, George Sampson!' shrieked Mrs Scrimshank. 'Don't think that I don't. You're being recorded on CCTV – I've got cameras in every room. I shall have you in jail for th–'

Mrs Scrimshank suddenly stopped talking as Boadicea pushed her muzzle right in her face.

'Listen, my old china,' said Boadicea in her most menacing tone. 'I think it might be best if you kept the old cakehole zipped shut for the time being.'

Mrs Scrimshank froze in shock. She was absolutely petrified. She simply couldn't believe what she'd seen and *heard*. In a stuttering voice she mumbled, 'A talking pony!'

'Well done – that's given the game away, hasn't it?' said Mr Nutcase sarcastically.

'And a talking squirrel,' jabbered Mrs Scrimshank, looking even more surprised.

Mr Nutcase buried his face in his paws. **'Doh!'** On the desk Jack saw a computer showing images from the security cameras inside the hotel: the badgers were now racing around the dining room, playing a game of chase with two breakfast trolleys, spilling eggs, beans and sausages as they went. The wild boars were charging up and down the corridors and pushing furniture down the stairs for fun.

Then Jack spotted a strange line in the floor, poking out from under the desk.

'Grandad, look!'

he shouted, pointing.

'Good lad,' said Grandad. 'Help me push.'

Grandad, Jack and Boadicea heaved the desk back to reveal a trapdoor beneath. Grandad lifted it open, and they all stood back in complete amazement at what they saw below. It was like an Aladdin's cave of riches that sparkled and glittered.

Grandad and Jack slowly crept down the small, steep staircase and looked in wonder at the treasure trove of riches.

Each precious item was displayed in its own glass case, with its own spotlight, and beside each was a little card:

Lady Anstruther
Diamond ring

Mrs Carmichael
Egyptian bracelet

Marquess McNurdoe
Emerald necklace

Mrs Scrimshank had obviously been stealing from her guests for years and years, just to add their valuables to her secret collection, to lock them up like the Crown Jewels.

'And look here!' said Jack, pointing to a box of computer disks in the corner.

Grandad looked inside. 'These must be disks from the actual days she stole things. They've got dates on and everything. Blimey, it'll take us ages to go through this lot. Unless you know the actual date of the theft your mum was accused of . . . '

Jack thought back to all the prison visits he'd made and the words echoed in his head. He could almost see his mother saying them: '*It was the first of April – April Fool's Day – I thought it was a joke at first, but it turned into a horrible nightmare,*' he repeated.

Grandad flicked through the disks. 'The first of April last year. Ah, here it is. Let's check it.'

They climbed out of the secret room and slipped the disk into the computer on the desk. Mrs Scrimshank's eyes opened even wider in alarm, but she was too flabbergasted to say anything.

'Look at her, just gawping like that,' said Mr Nutcase. 'And they have the nerve to call themselves the masters of the world!'

'Don't be too hard on her, old bean,' said Boadicea. 'Perhaps she's trying to catch a fly.'

Grandad pressed the FAST FORWARD button, and everyone watched the screen with great interest. Recordings from all the cameras flashed by in a patchwork of images, and the one in the top right-hand corner showed what had happened in the staff changing room on the first of April. It was full of lockers, and the staff came in at intervals, changed into their work clothes and left.

'There!' shouted Jack. 'That's my mum!'

Grandad slowed the images down to normal speed and they watched as Jack's mum opened her locker, put her coat and her handbag inside it, slipped on her chambermaid's overall and left the room.

'Well, now we know which locker is hers,' said Grandad, pressing FAST FORWARD again. They watched for a while as people came and went, and then suddenly someone appeared at Jack's mum's locker and left again very quickly.

'Rewind that bit!' shouted Jack.

Grandad wound it back and slowed the images to normal speed. There on the screen was Mrs Scrimshank. They watched as she used one of the keys on her enormous key ring to open Jack's mum's locker. She carefully took the diamond necklace out of her own pocket and dropped it into Jack's mum's handbag, then locked the door and slunk away.

Grandad wound the CCTV back once more and paused on the image of her dropping the necklace into Jack's mum's bag. Then everyone in the room turned to look at Mrs Scrimshank.

'It *was* you!'

they all shouted at once.

She said nothing, but her face slowly twisted into a look of complete madness.

'Well, my dear woman,' said Boadicea, 'what do you have to say for yourself?'

'Animals . . . Talking animals,' wittered Mrs Scrimshank, her brain struggling to comprehend what she was seeing. She began to dribble and laugh, and cast her eyes about the room like a madwoman.

'Oh dear,' said Mr Nutcase. 'I think she's losing her marbles.'

'I'm minded to agree with you, Mr Nutcase,' said Boadicea. 'She's going completely doolally.'

Right at that moment they heard police sirens screeching up the drive.

'I think it's time for us to leave,' said Mr Nutcase to Jack and Grandad. 'You have your evidence. I suggest you hand it over to the police. They're only human, of course, but I'm sure they'll do their best. Now mind your ears while I sound the tactical retreat.'

Grandad and Jack covered their ears.

OoOCHIIIKAAA!!!!!!!'

screamed Mr Nutcase.

By the time the police pulled up in front of
the hotel, got out of their vehicles and entered
the building, all the animals except Boadicea had
vanished. It was as if they had never been there
at all. The only ones left were a beaming Jack
and Grandad, and a gibbering wreck called Mrs
Scrimshank.

And a line of hedgehogs, led by Mr Snufflepants,
slowly inching their way towards the hotel door.

CHAPTER

18

The judge at the local court was very busy over the next few weeks. The first thing she did was cancel Jack's mum's prison sentence.

'Bridget Elizabeth Sampson,' said the judge, from behind an enormous desk in the courtroom, 'you have been the victim of a great injustice for which we are all deeply, deeply sorry. You are free to go immediately.'

Jack's mum rushed across the courtroom and scooped Jack up into her arms. She smothered him with hugs and kisses while everyone in the courtroom cheered and threw their hats in the air.

'Oh, my beautiful little boy,' she said, 'how I've missed you! I promise I'll never spend another day without you.'

Normally Jack would have just smiled and hugged her back and said nothing at all, but everything that had happened to him over the past few days had made him feel much bolder and more confident.

'I love you, Mum,' he said.

She looked at him in great surprise, as he'd never said this before, and her heart almost broke with happiness.

'What did you just say?' she asked.

'I love you, I love you, I love you,' said Jack as the pair of them danced around the courtroom.

Next up in court was Mrs Scrimshank. The judge took a very dim view of how she had framed Jack's mum. The court also heard from seventy-three former workers at the hotel, including Grandad, who had been sacked without holiday pay for crimes that Mrs Scrimshank had simply made up.

Mrs Scrimshank didn't say much in her own defence. In fact, she spent the whole time she was in the dock just rocking backwards and forwards, dribbling, occasionally bursting into hysterical laughter and mumbling, 'A talking horse . . . a talking squirrel . . .'

She had been examined by psychologists, who said that she was suffering from hallucinations and that she'd been hearing voices – animal voices in particular – and that she was, in their opinion, seriously ill and a danger to society.

The judge ordered her to be sent to a secure mental hospital until she was well enough to be sentenced properly. She requisitioned the hotel and entrusted it to Jack's mum, his grandad and the other seventy-two workers who had been treated so badly.

Everyone in the courtroom cheered and threw their hats in the air again, and some of them didn't get the right one back for weeks.

The third person up in court was Jack's cousin Kelly.

Jack thought she should have been arrested for bad acting because, once he'd given himself up to the police, the local papers and TV stations went a bit crazy and interviewed Kelly in the flat. In the interview she showed them the cupboard where Jack slept.

'He was basically my best friend,' she said, crying crocodile tears. 'In fact, I actually worshipped him. I loved him so much that I let him have my big bedroom all to himself while I slept here in this mouse-infested cupboard with the mop and bucket.'

The clip went viral on the internet because, if you looked very carefully, you could see some mice on a shelf behind her and they seemed to be shaking their heads in an *I can't believe she thinks she can get away with this* sort of way. One of the mice was half hidden by a camera sitting on the shelf and looked as if he was taking a picture of her.

But she wasn't in court for her bad acting. She was in court for theft. Uncle Ted had been sent some pictures, anonymously, that showed Kelly stealing his football programmes. His collection was now completely ruined. He found that she'd pinched more than a hundred of the most valuable ones over the last year and had been selling them cheaply to other collectors.

Aunt Violet begged Uncle Ted not to press charges, but he insisted, and Cousin Kelly was sentenced to six months in a young offender institution.

Although, during the trial, Uncle Ted was ordered out of the courtroom by the judge for '*secretly playing the trumpet*'.

Aunt Violet was so unhappy that Uncle Ted could send their own daughter to prison that she packed her bags and left him the same day.

After hearing how he'd treated Jack, Jack's mum wished that Uncle Ted could be sent to prison too. Grandad told her that just being a horrible, mean, cantankerous old man wasn't a crime. But Boadicea thought she could help . . .

And, from that day forward, whenever Uncle Ted went to a football match, he would be harassed by seagulls. They would steal his pie and eat his

chips, and best
of all, they would
poo on his head.

On his way there and
back, dogs would
cock their legs and
wee on him in
the street, and if he
happened to pass any cats they
would 'spray' him.

At home the mice would steal the remote
control for the TV and change channels while he
was watching his favourite programme. And when
he went to sleep at night they kept switching the
lights on and off so that he never got any proper
rest.

CHAPTER

19

As well as being given a share of the hotel by the
judge, Jack's mum was also awarded a lot of money
as compensation for being wrongly imprisoned, but
the biggest windfall of all came to Jack.

When the lawyers read Old Mr Mudge's will,
they found that he had left absolutely everything to
'the closest thing to family I has ever had – young
Jack'.

The junkyard was worth an enormous sum
of money, not as a business but because the land
itself was extremely valuable. It was very close to
the centre of town, and Jack and his mum sold
it to the town council, who built a new park with

a big splashy fountain in the middle. It was one
of those dancing fountains, like a pavement with
jets of water that would shoot up into the air in
sequence. It was fun to run around it trying not to
get wet, and it was a big hit with all the children in
the town. As part of the contract, Jack insisted that
they call the park 'Mudge Park'.

With the money from the sale, Jack and his mum
bought Broadacre Farm.

They decided that, instead of having a normal
farm with cows and sheep, they would run it as
a sanctuary for horses and ponies who had come
upon hard times.

'Lord preserve us from the glue factory,'
whispered Boadicea with a shudder.

They asked Grandad to come and help run the
place, and they filled the stable yard and the fields
with delightful characters from far and wide: old
ponies who had become rather unloved; racehorses
who had developed a limp; working horses who

could no longer work; and even a couple of seaside donkeys who had had enough of the beach.

Jack and Boadicea decided it would be best
if no one else knew that she could talk. It was
their secret, and like all secrets it made the bond
between them even stronger. Jack's mum could see
that they had a very close friendship; she thought
that was good for Jack and made him more
confident.

Boadicea lived in the nearest stable to the house
and kept all the horses in order. She told them how
Jack had saved her from the knacker's yard, that he
knew they could talk, that they could all trust him
and, perhaps most importantly, that he was always
good for an extra scoop of pony nuts!

A rather fine old mare called Jemima had been
a carriage horse for a retired schoolteacher. When
the schoolteacher died of old age, Jemima decided
to come and live at Broadacre Farm. She was a
wise old girl and had picked up a lot of knowledge
from living with the schoolteacher.

She watched Jack struggling to read the
instructions on a bottle of hoof oil one day and

realized that he was dyslexic. Without making him feel self-conscious about it, she helped Jack read the instructions on everything after that, and pretty soon he was bringing his homework into her stable to get help.

They would read stories together, and Jemima encouraged Jack to read out loud and make pictures of the words in his head as he was reading. They would chat about the story and the pictures in his head, and make jokes and read it over again . . . and soon afterwards Jack was going to school with a spring in his step, feeling more positive about what the day might throw at him.

Aunt Violet also came to live with Jack and his mum – back to the place she and Bridget had called home when they were children. The two sisters absolutely loved it. Only a day after she moved in, all the colour returned to Aunt Violet's face and she stopped sniffing! The coughs, colds and sneezes disappeared and never returned.

She bought a cookbook and learned to make the most scrumptious meals. She got so good at cooking that Grandad planted lots of fruit bushes – raspberries, strawberries and blueberries – and she started making jam. The jam was so tasty that

she opened a small farm shop, and people came
from miles around to buy it. So she started selling
delicious tarts, cakes and biscuits too.

It really was the happiest place in the world to live.

CHAPTER

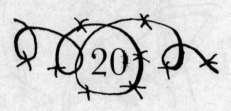

The only person who wasn't happy for Jack and his mum was Joe Sampson.

Things had gone from bad to worse at the Joe Sampson Riding Stables. Joe had gambled all his money away. The yard was now a complete wreck. All the grooms and stable hands had left because he was so cruel to them, and all the horses had gone except Morning Glory.

Morning Glory was Joe's only hope – she was a really good racehorse. She was going to run in the Grand National and, although she wasn't the favourite to win, she was *in* the race, so there was a chance, and if she *did* win Joe would be a rich man again . . . But the racecourse was a long way away and Joe couldn't even afford the petrol to get there in the horsebox.

Joe decided that he would try to get the money for the petrol from Jack. *After all,* he thought to himself, *he is my son!*

And he came up with a plan: he was sure that Jack wouldn't be able to resist the chance to have a little ride on a horse that was going to run in the Grand National. So he invited Jack round and, despite Grandad's reservations, the next day Jack, Grandad and Boadicea turned up at the Joe Sampson Riding Stables.

Joe rushed out to greet them.

'Oh look, here's my *son*, my lovely *son*, my *son* who I happen to be the *father* of. How lovely to see you, my . . .' Joe knew that nice parents said something like *little chicken* or *little sweet pea*, but he couldn't remember which, so after a pause he said, 'My little hen bean.'

Jack didn't know what to say. This was such a different Joe to the one who had shouted,

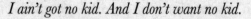
I ain't got no kid. And I don't want no kid.

'I bet you wanna see Morning Glory, don't you?' said Joe. 'Well, here she is.' And he brought her out of her stable.

She really was a magnificent-looking horse. Her coat gleamed, her ears were pricked, and she was lean and athletic, with a relaxed, long stride. She had an attitude of importance about her – she held her head high as if to say, *I'm the best.*

'Would you like a little ride on her, son? Even walking she'll be a lot quicker than that fat old Shetland you've got there.'

Boadicea gave him a savage look.

'If you could see your way to helping me out with some petrol money, and if I won the race, I could get you a much better horse,' said Joe.

'Boadicea's not just a horse,' said Jack. 'She's my best friend.'

'The only point of a horse is speed,' said Joe. 'Why don't I fetch you some proper racing clothes? Then you'll look the part as well.'

He scampered off into the Portakabin.

'I think racing's very overrated,' said Boadicea. 'All they do is go round in a circle and end up in the same place – what's the point of that? You'd get there just as fast – in fact, faster – just staying in the same place. You're already there! So why race at all?'

Morning Glory whinnied loudly and gave Boadicea a hard stare.

'Oh, it's all right,' said Boadicea. 'They've both been signed up to the animal code, haven't you?'

'That's right,' said Jack and Grandad, and they raised their right hands and said: '*Eeahu scree ki kaka, sker pwick ti cho!*'

'Well, why didn't you say?' said Morning Glory. 'Shhh! He's coming back.'

'I couldn't find any of the stable lad's gear, so you'll have to wear some of mine, but it might be a bit big for you,' said Joe, returning with some jodhpurs, riding boots, racing silks and a helmet with goggles.

'He's not that much smaller than you, Joe,' said Grandad.

Jack couldn't believe he was putting on actual racing gear. He remembered all those Saturdays sitting on the arm of Uncle Ted's chair in his pyjamas, and here he was wearing the real thing.

'Well, what do you know?' said Grandad. 'He looks the spitting image of you, Joe.'

'Right, up you get,' said Joe, giving Jack a lift up on to Morning Glory's back. 'Let's go out on to the gallops and you can have a proper little trot around.'

They went out on to the gallops behind the stables. It was like a private bit of racecourse. It had white rails on either side, just like a real racecourse, and two practice jumps.

'It's a bit overgrown, isn't it, Joe?' said Grandad.

'I had to sell the mower,' said Joe. 'Times are hard.'

'And it's full of rabbit holes,' added Grandad.

'Well, I need a bit of investment, you see,' said Joe. 'Perhaps young Jack here, my son, my very rich son, might go into business with me?'

Jack wasn't really listening: he was so excited to be on a real racehorse. Morning Glory trotted up and down, and even broke into a canter. Jack had to admit to himself that it was a much smoother ride than sitting on Boadicea's back.

'Please don't go too fast,' Jack whispered in Morning Glory's ear. 'I've never been on a real racehorse before and I'm a bit scared of falling off.'

'Relax – you'll only come off if I want you to,' Morning Glory whispered back. 'Let's go a little faster – I love speed.'

'You just stay out in the middle of the course, son!' shouted Joe from the side. 'We don't want Morning Glory putting a foot in a rabbit hole and breaking a leg.'

But, just as he finished speaking, Joe accidentally put his own foot into a hidden rabbit hole, and as he fell forward there was a loud

'Argghh! My ankle! My ankle! I've broken it!' he screamed.

Grandad ran over and bent down to examine Joe's ankle.

'It's not broken,' he said. 'It's just a really bad sprain – look, it's swelling up already.'

'But it's the race tomorrow and now I won't be able to ride! It was my only chance! Everything's ruined!' wailed Joe.

Grandad heard the steady beat of hooves and looked up to see Morning Glory galloping steadily along the course with Jack on her back.

'Well, will you look at that?' he said. 'With his goggles on, he looks just like you.'

Morning Glory was flying up the track. It was like everything Jack had ever imagined, but ten times as good. It was so smooth it felt like her feet weren't even touching the ground, but Jack could hear the *ba-da-da ba-da-da ba-da-da* of the hooves and the air whistling past his ears.

'They're headed for the jump – they'll never make it!' shouted Joe.

'Oh no! I've never done a jump before!' cried

Jack as the massive brushwood fence loomed larger and larger. 'It's too big! Please stop!'

'You just sit back and enjoy yourself,' said Morning Glory. 'I've got you. And I love jumping. Here we go!'

And she jumped . . .

Jack thought it was like being in a rocket. Morning Glory launched herself into the air and they sailed over quite serenely. Jack barely felt the landing at all as they galloped on to the next one.

Grandad and Joe watched with their mouths hanging open. They could hardly believe their eyes.

'He's a natural,' said Grandad. 'By God, he's a natural! I tell you what, Joe – *he* could ride her in the race tomorrow.'

'But what about the Jockey Club rules?' said Joe. 'You've gotta be at least sixteen to ride in the race.'

'But they'll just think it's you,' said Grandad. 'No one would ever know.'

They watched as Jack and Morning Glory reached the second jump and flew over it even more gracefully.

'Oh please, please, let it be true,' said Joe. 'He's so good. He's even better than me. This could work. He could win. He could. He could win the race!'

CHAPTER

The next day Jack travelled to the famous Aintree
Racecourse near Liverpool with Grandad, Mum,
Aunt Violet and Morning Glory. They had to leave
Joe at the stables, otherwise people would realize
that Jack wasn't him. And Boadicea stayed at
Broadacre Farm, where she and all the other horses
in the sanctuary were watching the race on a TV
that had been set up in the stable yard.

Jack wore his racing silks with his helmet and
his goggles at all times, so that he could pretend to
be Joe, and Grandad went around telling all the
people who knew Joe that he had a bad cold and
had lost his voice.

At last the time came to trot down to the starting

line. There were forty horses in the race, but Morning Glory managed to find a bit of space on the way over to have a private chat with Jack.

'Now, Jack,' she said, 'whereabouts in the race would you like to come?'

'Well, I'd like to win, of course,' said Jack.

'Everyone says that,' said Morning Glory. 'But do you *really* want to win?'

'I've watched this race on the TV every year since I was a baby,' said Jack. 'I've ridden it in my dreams so many times. I've practised it on the arm of my uncle's chair, on the side of the bath, on the ironing board, and I've even burned my bum doing it on a hot radiator. It's all I've ever wanted to do and I think this might be my only chance.'

'In that case we shall win,' said Morning Glory.

'Don't you mean "we'll *try* to win"?' asked Jack.

'No, we *shall* win,' said Morning Glory, then after a pause she added: 'You *do* know that we horses always discuss the race beforehand and decide?'

'**No!**' said Jack, aghast.

'Oh yes. We like to put on a show, of course, and we like to make it unpredictable so that the humans can play their silly guessing games, but really we just do it for the exercise. You watch.'

The horses and riders all gathered together near the starting line – a long tape held across the track – and Jack could hear the horses making noises: nickers, neighs and whinnies. They were talking to each other in horse language.

Morning Glory talked the most, and when she'd finished all the other horses looked at Jack, and he thought some of them smiled and others nodded their heads and one of them even winked at him.

'Hey, Joe,' said another rider. 'You've forgotten your whip.'

'Oh, I don't use a whip – horses respond best to kindness,' said Jack, before suddenly remembering that he shouldn't talk, in case he gave the game away.

'That doesn't sound like you, Joe,' replied the jockey.

'Well, I've had a bad cold,' said Jack in the deepest voice he could manage.

'No, I mean not using a whip – you usually flog 'em to death!'

All the other riders laughed.

'Doesn't sound like your voice either,' said another rider.

But before Jack had to answer, the starter shouted into his megaphone, 'Steady!'

They all looked round, the tape went up and they were off!

The next nine minutes were the most exciting of Jack's life. He felt like he was in a dream, racing towards the first fence with thirty-nine other horses and riders – the noise was tremendous, as if hundreds of drummers were banging on big bass drums.

Up and over they went, with Jack feeling like they'd been fired from a cannon, but they landed safely on the other side and carried on.

Fence after fence they jumped, with the other horses galloping alongside, some of them looking up at Jack and giving him a little flick of the head in encouragement.

The sixth fence was a jump called Becher's Brook, which was higher on the take-off side than it was on the landing side.

'Lean right back!'

shouted Morning Glory as they took off. Jack did as he was told and they landed comfortably on the other side. But two of the other horses used it as an opportunity to get rid of their riders, laughing as they did so.

The next big jump was called the Canal Turn, and Jack looked to his right, just beyond the racecourse, and saw a canal stretching out into the distance.

That must be the canal Old Mr Mudge was talking about, he thought to himself. *It must lead right back to Mudge Park.*

He imagined how proud Old Mr Mudge would have been to see him racing along now.

Morning Glory was in the middle of the field of horses, galloping along very comfortably.

'I thought we were going to win,' said Jack into her ear.

'Plenty of time for that,' she replied. 'Remember we have to give the humans a bit of entertainment. They don't like it when a horse just stays at the front all the time. They like the winner to come from behind.'

The race was twice around the course, and as they came to the end of the first lap they passed four enormous grandstands full of people.

'So many people!' said Jack.

'Oh yes,' said Morning Glory. 'About a hundred and fifty thousand in the stands, but I believe the TV audience is six hundred million around the

world. Which is why we like to look our best. Wave
as you go past.'

Jack threw his hand into the air as they thundered
by – and the crowd responded with a mighty cheer.

They set off on the second lap.

'Time for a bit of fun, I think,' said Morning
Glory. 'You tell me which rider you'd like to fall off
next.'

Jack looked up with a big grin on his face.

'What about that one in the blue-and-red
stripes?' he said.

'Right you are,' said Morning Glory, and she
made a loud whinnying squeal to the horse ahead.

As they reached the next jump, the horse
suddenly stopped in its tracks, and the jockey in the
blue-and-red stripes shot off into the air and landed
right in the hedge.

Jack laughed.

'That's incredible!'

'Yes, it is quite fun, isn't it? Who next?'

Jack spent the next four jumps deciding who
would fall off and laughing like a drain when their
horses catapulted them into a ditch or threw them
over a fence. He looked back at the fallen riders to
see them waving their fists in the air and stamping
the ground in frustration.

'This is my personal favourite – it's called
"broken girth",' said Morning Glory.

She nickered and neighed to a horse galloping
alongside. The horse turned and smiled at Jack,
then she blew her tummy out as far as it would go,
snapping the girth strap that held the saddle on,
and the poor rider simply slid off sideways.

Even Morning Glory laughed at that one.

'Right, time to get serious,' she said. 'This is the run-in to the finishing post. Hold on tight!'

Jack nearly fell off backwards as she suddenly zoomed away. She was going nearly twice as fast as before. The crowd went crazy. There were still ten other horses and riders in front of her, but with each stride she was gaining on them. She passed one, then another, and the third smiled at Jack as they thundered by.

There were only a hundred metres to go now. Morning Glory passed another four horses in just two strides, and then she had the leading pack of three in her sights.

'Goodness gracious, they're cutting it rather fine!' she puffed, but Jack could hardly hear her because of the roar of the crowd.

Onwards and onwards she raced, the cheers and the shouting lifting her as she went. With fifty metres to go, she reached the first of the remaining horses; another stride and she was past.

Two to go. On she thundered. Jack bent down low like he'd seen the other jockeys do.

Twenty-five metres to go and Morning Glory thought it might be too much, but with an enormous effort she stretched her legs out even further – and she was on them.

At fifteen metres she was level with the next horse. At ten she caught up with the leader. Maybe she wouldn't make it . . . but no – one last extra push and she was through and they'd won!

Jack had never heard so much noise. One hundred and fifty thousand people in the stands erupted into a cacophony of jubilation. They'd never seen a Grand National as close as this before – it was truly a wonder.

Jack felt an intense kind of happiness he'd never felt before. His whole body tingled with joy. He hugged Morning Glory's neck and said, 'Thank you, thank you, thank you! That was the best thing that's ever happened to me.'

The race was over, but the crowd kept on

cheering, and they cheered Jack and Morning
Glory all the way to the winner's enclosure – which
was where the winning horse and trainer went to
collect the prize money and an enormous cup.

Grandad, Mum and Aunt
Violet were there, all sobbing
their eyes out in happiness.
Back at Penny Bridges, Joe
Sampson was jumping up and
down for joy in his little
Portakabin, even though
his ankle was tightly
bandaged and he was in a lot
of pain.
And at Broadacre
Farm the horses
watching in the
stable yard were
cheering for all they
were worth. Boadicea
did a special jig on

her back legs, spinning round and round until she fell over with joy.

Back at the racecourse Grandad, as the trainer of the horse, was being given a cheque for the prize money and the big cup. Everyone clapped, and then a man with a microphone asked Grandad to say a few words.

Grandad paused. He looked at the crowd. He looked at Jack's mum and Aunt Violet. And he looked at Jack, who was beaming from ear to ear.

But a look of sadness crossed Grandad's face, and at length he took hold of the microphone.

'I could stand here today and accept this prize and this cup, and none of you would ever be any the wiser . . .'

The crowd hushed – this wasn't the kind of thing they were expecting to hear.

'But the truth is, if I did that, you would all think that my son Joe was a champion jockey. And he's not a champion jockey. He's not a champion anything. I'll tell you exactly what he is – he's a mean-spirited, cruel and heartless good-for-nothing. He's cruel to horses and to people. He'd never lift a finger to help anyone else. And I don't want you all going away today thinking that he's a good sort . . .'

Everyone turned their attention to Jack.

'. . . because my eyes have been opened by someone who is good. Someone who is kind. The kindest soul I know. Someone who has gone through a lot of hardship in his young life, but who is still kind. He's kind to humans, but he's especially kind to horses. In fact, he's kinder to horses than anybody else you'll ever meet. And I know we've broken the Jockey Club rules by letting him ride in this race, and I know we'll have to give up the prize and the cup, but I'm just so very proud of him that I couldn't let this moment go without telling you all. Ladies and gentlemen, let me introduce you to my grandson – Jack!'

The crowd broke into gasps of wonder and awe, which slowly turned into applause and cheers, and pretty soon they were giving Jack a standing ovation and shouting,

'Hurrah!'

at the tops of their voices. They were clapping and waving and throwing their hats in the air.

Though one man – who'd already lost a hat during the court case – was rather annoyed to find that he'd lost his hat again, and that all he was left with was a pink bonnet covered in silk flowers.

The Jockey Club did disqualify Morning Glory and Jack, but it only made them even more famous. Not only had a young boy actually won the most important race in the world, he'd done it on a horse that wasn't expected to win. Jack and Morning Glory were all over the TV news – it was the most remarkable result of the Grand National ever. A film company even wanted to make a movie of his life!

CHAPTER

When Jack and Grandad returned Morning Glory
to Joe's stables, they were worried that Joe might
be furious with them, but he seemed very calm. In
fact, he appeared to be in some sort of trance.

'How did you do it, son?' asked Joe quietly.
'How did you do it? I know that horse. I know it's
good – but it's not that good. So how did you do it,
son? Did you bribe the other riders? Did you drug
the other horses? What did you do?'

'I just asked her,' said Jack. 'Very kindly.'

'You asked her very kindly?' said Joe
incredulously. 'Just *asked* her?'

'Yes,' said Jack, his mind going back to the time
he'd spent at the junkyard. 'Old Mr Mudge used to

say that horses are like humans – they respond best to a bit of kindness.'

'It's true, Joe,' said Grandad. 'That's all it was – no bribing or anything like that – just being kind.'

'Just being kind . . . if only I'd tried that earlier,' said Joe softly. 'Who's Old Mr Mudge?'

'He was a kind old man, Joe,' said Grandad. 'The man with the junkyard. He acted like a father to young Jack here. Because no one else would.'

Joe turned slowly to Grandad.

'You were right in what you said,' he told him. 'Now that I've lost everything I can see myself much more clearly. I *have* been cruel and heartless and mean. And because of that I've lost all my money, I've lost everyone's respect, I've lost my friends, and I've even lost the stables because I've borrowed so much that the bank will sell them to get their money back. But the thing I regret losing the most,' he said, turning to Jack, 'is the son I never knew I had. I'm sorry I wasn't there for you. I'm genuinely sorry. And I can see now that it's all too late. But, wherever life leads me now, I'll bear in mind what you said. I'll try a bit of kindness from now on.'

And he turned and walked away.

'Orses is like humans; they respond best to a bit of kindness – Old Mr Mudge's words were echoing round and round in Jack's head.

Well, that meant that humans needed kindness too, didn't it?

'Wait!' shouted Jack, but Joe kept on walking. 'Wait!' But Joe kept moving.

'Wait . . . Dad!'

Joe stopped and turned round. 'What did you call me?'

'Dad,' said Jack.

'After all that's happened you'll let me be your dad?'

'Only if you want to be.'

'Oh, son, I would love that. I would really love that.'

They slowly came together in the middle of the
yard and tentatively put their arms around each
other. It was a hug that grew stronger, firmer and
then tighter still, until they could hardly breathe,
but they were so happy they didn't care.

Against everyone else's advice, Jack bought the
stables to stop them being taken by the bank. He

brought back all the horses and the people who
had been working there, and he put Joe, his dad, in
charge. Because Jack thought that everyone should
have a second chance and he believed that his dad
had changed.

And Jack was RIGHT!

Joe stopped gambling and set to work. In
no time at all he had the stables completely
redecorated. All the stable doors were fixed,
the slates were put back on the roof, the ugly
Portakabin was taken away and the yard soon
looked like the best stable yard in the country. The
ravens disappeared and never returned.

The grooms and stable hands couldn't believe
the change in him – he was always ready for a
laugh, always happy to help – they really enjoyed
coming to work.

Even the horses were surprised.

'We can't believe what's come over him,' said
one of them to Boadicea. 'He feeds us properly,
he exercises us just right, he washes us down

afterwards, he can't do enough for us, and he's always so polite and respectful. He took all his whips and broke them in two and threw them on the bonfire!'

And Joe started winning! And, even if a horse didn't win, he didn't lose his temper. He just said, 'Never mind, you tried your best and that's all you can do.'

Joe was a different and a much happier man.

Jack was a different boy too. He was now much more outgoing. In fact, he was the kind of boy who found it hard to stop talking.

His mum liked to watch him and Boadicea from the kitchen window. She could see them across the field, larking about in their favourite spot under the oak tree. She couldn't hear them, but she knew something was going on between them.

They looked like a pair of best friends: nattering, acting out stories, falling about laughing and giving each other high fives.

She knew she wasn't supposed to know that
they could talk, but their secret was safe with her,
because it was one of the best sights in the world.

THE END

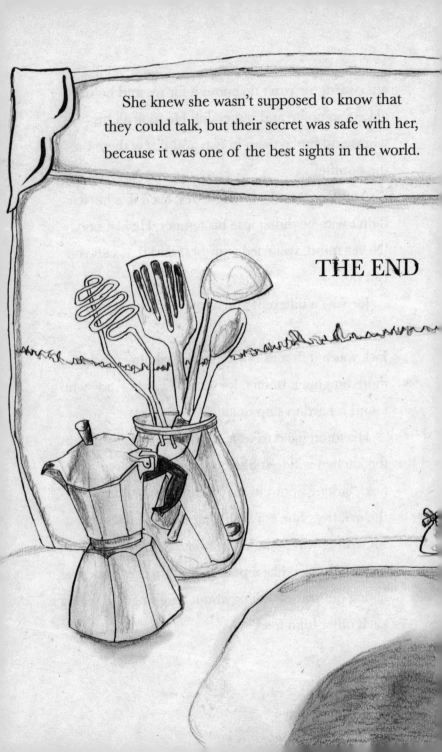

Also by Adrian Edmondson

Have you read . . .

CHAPTER

1

In the middle of the night there was a loud

explosion.

Tilly woke up with a start. At first she didn't know whether the bang she'd heard was part of a dream or something that had happened in real life.

She lay under her duvet looking this way and that, trying to see things in her dark bedroom. She really wanted to find out what had made the noise, but it was a freezing cold night and she really didn't want to get out of bed.

Suddenly, through the gap in her thin curtains,

she saw a shower of sparks, which lit up her tiny bedroom. It was as if someone had set off a large firework just outside her window. In the light of the sparks she could see Big Tedder and Mr Fluffybunny sitting on the shelf at the end of her bed. She could also see her uniform laid out on the chair behind the door, ready for school in the morning. And she could see the big photo of her with her mummy and her dad, which she kept in a frame on her bedside table. The photo had been taken in the kitchen downstairs, and they all looked very happy.

Tilly's house was what her dad called an old-fashioned 'two up, two down', which meant it had two rooms upstairs and two rooms downstairs. Though this wasn't strictly true: there was just her bedroom and her dad's bedroom upstairs, but downstairs there was a living room, a kitchen *and* a new bit of house that stuck out at the back, which was their bathroom.

There was another explosion, much smaller this time – more like a *crump* – followed by a different-coloured shower of sparks. Tilly sniffed the air with her tiny button of a nose. Could she smell burning? She would have to get up and investigate.

She slid out of bed, dragging the duvet with her, wrapping it round her like a lovely warm cloak. She shuffled across to the window and looked out.

The bathroom took up most of the space in the small yard at the back of the house, but her dad had still managed to squeeze a shed into the corner. This was where he did his 'experiments'. Tilly's dad was a scientist, and he loved inventing things. He used to invent things for the government, but he didn't work for them any more. In fact he didn't work for anyone any more, so he did all his inventing in the shed at home.

As she looked out of her bedroom window, Tilly could see her dad through the window of the shed. He was leaping up and down, grinning from ear to ear, and it looked like half his beard was on fire.

He turned and saw her, and immediately ran out of the shed, patting his beard to extinguish the flames.

'Tilly! Tilly! Come down and look at this! My machine – it's working!'

'Wow!' said Tilly excitedly, although she didn't really know what the machine was. But she moved away from the window, dropped her duvet on the floor and started towards the door.

'No time for the stairs!' shouted her dad. 'Just jump out of the window – I'll catch you!'

Tilly couldn't believe her ears. She ran back to the window and flung it open. 'Are you sure?' she shouted.

'Yes, of course! You're only small – I'll catch you!'

Tilly didn't like being called small. She was seven and a half, which in her opinion was quite big. But in the excitement of the moment she couldn't be bothered to argue. She scrambled on to the windowsill and looked down at her dad. His hair always stood on end as if he had just electrocuted himself, and he was smiling the big cheerful smile he always smiled. His beard was still smouldering, and she could see that one of the lenses of his thick black glasses was broken.

He held out his arms, ready to catch her.

Tilly stood there in her pyjamas.

'I-I'm f-frightened,' she stammered.

'Don't be such a scaredy-cat! It's hardly any distance at all – come on!'

Tilly knew that if her mummy was still alive she wouldn't let her do anything like this. Tilly missed her very much, but if there was any good side at all to her mummy dying it was that she could do the crazy stuff her dad let her do, like jumping out of windows.

'Life is for living, Tilly, my love,' shouted her dad. 'You only live once!'

'Here I come!' she shouted back, and she jumped off the ledge and landed safely in his arms.

'That's my girl. Come and look at this,' said her dad, carrying her quickly to the shed.

It was quite a small shed, but it was jam-packed with machinery. There were wires everywhere, as if the whole place was full of brightly coloured spaghetti. Lights blinked, wheels turned, and some things just shook and gurgled.

'What is it?' asked Tilly.

'It's a time machine!' said her dad. 'They told me I'd never get it to work, but finally it does! This evening I've already been to visit Admiral Nelson at the Battle of Trafalgar, and to the 1966 World Cup Final. You wouldn't believe it – I met the German goalkeeper Hans Tilkowski *and* Geoff Hurst! He scored three goals for England, although some people think his third goal didn't actually cross the line.'

These things didn't mean much to Tilly, but she could see that they impressed her dad.

'Come on,' he said, twiddling some dials and tapping away at his computer keyboard. 'Where

would you like to go? You can go anywhere
you like at any time in history – although at the
moment I can only manage to stay there for a
minute or two, then I pop straight back . . .'

'Anywhere at all?' asked Tilly.

'That's right, anywhere at all.'

'At any time I like?'

'At any time you like,' said her dad. 'You could
see a chariot race in ancient Rome, or travel with
the Pilgrim Fathers to America. Or – aren't you
doing a school project about Victorian England?
You could go there if you like.'

Tilly thought hard. She knew at once where
she wanted to go, but she was afraid to say, in case
her dad got upset.

'Come on,' he said enthusiastically. 'You
could see what life was really like for children
in Victorian times. You could even meet Queen
Victoria!' And he turned to his machine and
started typing in the details for Buckingham
Palace during the reign of Queen Victoria.

'I'd like to go back to my sixth birthday, when Mummy was still here,' said Tilly.

She didn't mean to say it aloud, but it just came out, because that's what she was thinking, and that's where she really wanted to go.

She knew her dad didn't like talking about her mummy, or the fact that she had died, because it made him sad.

He stopped what he was doing and sat very still for a moment. He sniffed hard a couple of times, and his eyes sparkled as if he was about to cry. Then he turned to Tilly. 'Are you sure you want to go back to your sixth birthday, my angel? Mummy was very poorly then, wasn't she?'

'But she was very smiley,' said Tilly. 'And that's when the photo was taken – the one I keep next to my bed; the one where everyone's laughing. It's the last photo of Mummy.'

Her dad took her in his arms and hugged her very tightly. 'Oh, Tilly, you're such a lovely little girl. Of course you want to see your

mummy. Why didn't I think of that?'

One of her dad's arms was wrapped right round her head, and Tilly could hear the loud ticking of the watch he wore on his wrist.

She liked her dad's watch because her mummy had given it to him the Christmas before she died. On the back it had an engraving that read:

TO MY DARLING JOHN,
I WILL LOVE YOU FOR ALL TIME,
LOVE JULIA X

It was a very special watch. Not only did it have an extra-loud tick but it could tell you the day and the date, and what time sunrise and sunset were going to be. It also worked as a compass. Her dad was very pleased when he got it, and he always wore it.